Burn Bright

The Night Creatures
Book One

Marianne de Pierres

Copyright © 2013, Marianne de Pierres

ISBN-10: 1482763273
ISBN-13: 978-1482763270

*For Mum, Dad, Nicci, Simon, Paul and Colleen.
(One phrase, Simon: Crawley traffic lights.)*

Contents

Part One: Retra   1

Chapter One   3
Chapter Two   13
Chapter Three   26
Chapter Four   34
Chapter Five   46
Chapter Six   56
Chapter Seven   66
Chapter Eight   82
Chapter Nine   94
Chapter Ten   106
Chapter Eleven   113
Chapter Twelve   126
Chapter Thirteen   135
Chapter Fourteen   139
Chapter Fifteen   145
Chapter Sixteen   157
Chapter Seventeen   162
Chapter Eighteen   167

Part Two: Naif	171
Chapter Nineteen	173
Chapter Twenty	180
Chapter Twenty-One	186
Chapter Twenty-Two	204
Chapter Twenty-Three	221
Chapter Twenty-Four	230
Chapter Twenty-Five	238
Chapter Twenty-Six	249
About the Author	261
Acknowledgements	262

part one

retra

one

Retra pressed her fingers to her thigh. The intense pain from her obedience strip had receded to a steady throb and nausea. Perhaps that was the worst it would get, now that she'd left the compound.

She glanced back. No shout came. No lights followed her. The rust-mesh fence that segregated the Seal enclave from the rest of Grave rose like a grey fortress in the dark. And she'd climbed it.

Pain can be dismissed.

Her brother Joel had said that to her after Father had beat him one time. Retra remembered that more clearly than anything after he ran away to Ixion. It was the thing that gave her hope. She could control pain. And she could follow him.

So she'd practised. Hours with her arm twisted, or something sharp pressed into her skin; practised thinking and acting, despite hurt.

And now was the time.

The barge would be waiting at the old harbour ramp where the tugs brought in the coal haulers. Down among the filthy, rat-infested dockside streets she'd find her escape.

Others drifted close as she hurried through the city streets towards the water. She heard their boots on cobblestones, and their quick, heavy breaths rasping the damp air. Hurrying like her.

Don't miss it! It's here!

The barge comes twice a year, sneaking in under the cover of night, taking the unhappy ones away to Ixion, Joel had told her. *No one knows when it will arrive. That's why the Elders can't stop it. The confetti falls. We read it but only we know the code.*

What code? Retra had said. *I don't know a code.*

The Angel Arias *are the code.*

What's Ixion? she'd asked him.

He'd laid his face close to hers, whispering so their parents couldn't hear. *Imagine a place where there are no Elders. No rules. No punishment. Only music and laughter and freedom. That's Ixion, Ret. That's me.*

Soon after, he'd run away and left her alone.

Fog licked Retra's face as she ran but she barely felt the chill. The pain was back. Waves of throbbing making her slow down and double over. She gasped for breath, staggered a few steps then kept moving, keeping to the side of the street, letting others pass.

She mustn't stop now. If Father found her here, he'd beat her unconscious. There was no forgiveness for Ixion runaways who were caught. Only rebuke and shame.

But the throbbing radiated along her leg and up into her abdomen, making the world contract. The decrepit buildings seemed to sag towards her; the cobblestones became too large and uneven to balance upon.

She stopped again and brushed her veil aside to catch a deeper breath. Ahead, a string of shifting party lights lit the outline of the barge. She just had to get across the street and down the beach to the ramp. That's all.

One foot. Follow. One foot. Follow.

Across the deserted street.

But as her boots touched sand, the boat engine rumbled into life and the drawbridge began to close.

Wait ... please wait ...

Ignoring the crippling pain, she ran the last few steps and flung herself at the closing gate. If she fell short of the barge she would die: the chill, dark water would suck her clothes-laden body down.

If she fell short, maybe it would be best to die.

Her arms slapped the lip of the drawbridge, her fingers missing their grip, and she began to slide.

No!

Then strong, cold hands dragged her up and into the safety of the boat. But her moment of relief ebbed as she stared up at her rescuer. Pale as a dead person alive, eyes cold, hair flowing long and blacker than the night she'd run through to get here, skin tight and gaunt across the bones of his face like a skeleton clinging to its flesh.

'Welcome aboard the way to Ixion: island of ever-night, ever-youth and never-sleep. Burn bright!' He gave her a mock salute and disappeared along the long, shadowy deck towards the bridge, leaving her shivering over what she had done.

At least the pain from her strip had ebbed, as if his icy hands had robbed it of heat. She could breathe again.

'Do you think they're all like that?'

Jerked from her thoughts, Retra searched for the owner of the voice. It belonged to a girl huddled into the side of the hull against the damp dark and the strangeness. Straight blonde hair spilled past the girl's shoulders. Retra had never seen hair quite so white. She wanted to touch it to see if it was real or made of moonlight.

'All who?' she asked instead, crouching among the shadows near her.

'The Ripers.'

'What's a Riper?'

'Don't you read the confetti?' asked the girl.

Retra thought of the balloon gondola that floated across from Ixion sometimes and littered Grave's wet, stone streets with flyers. Father had whipped her for picking them up. Then he had burnt them in the wood stove. But Joel had smuggled a flyer home and whispered to her about it. 'Yes. Once.'

The girl sighed as if Retra was an idiot. 'Ripers are the Guardians of Ixion. They look after you. They know everything. Even when you're too old to live there anymore.'

'What happens to you then?'

The girl shrugged as if she didn't care, but Retra could see the glittering excitement in her eyes, coloured by the party lights that wound around the ship's railing.

'How should I know? That's ages away for me.' She gave a wicked smile. 'I'm only seventeen. I've got a lot of partying to do before then.'

Retra's stomach tightened. 'I've never been to a party.'

The girl stuck a finger in her mouth and sucked it. 'None of us have. But I've been practising what to say if a cute guy wants me to dance. Or go somewhere with him.' She tittered. 'Anyway, I'm Cal. What's your name?'

Hesitantly, Retra leaned into the shifting coloured light and lifted her veil. 'I'm Retra.'

Cal's smile faded. She wrinkled her nose. 'I didn't see your veil. You're a *Seal*. They don't like Seals in Ixion, it takes them too long to loosen up. Some of them go frossing mad before they do.'

Retra stiffened. Cal's swearing shocked her. 'How do you know that?'

Cal inched away as if she might catch something. 'Stands to reason, doesn't it? You super-straights are a bit retarded. Give you some freedom and you "snap".' She clicked her fingers. 'Some go into themselves, others go wild – that's what I've heard. Wonder which sort you'll be?'

Super-straights. Is that what the rest of Grave called them?

Well, Cal might know how to swear but she didn't know anything about Retra. Seals didn't just live in sealed compounds. They lived in sealed minds. The first thing a Seal child learnt was how to shield her thoughts and emotions from others.

That's why Retra missed Joel so much. Only with her brother could she whisper secrets. Only with him did she feel safe to share her feelings. 'We aren't retarded,' she said. 'We are ...' She searched for the word. 'Private.'

'Is that why you don't go to school or to Council meets? Is that why you live in that stupid compound? 'Cos you're *private*.'

Cal's sarcasm made Retra nervous. 'We attend Face-School,' she said.

'Face-School's weird, just talking to a teacher-head on a square box.'

'It's a proven way to learn.'

'*Proven way to learn*,' mimicked Cal. 'School's not about learning. It's about friends. Everyone knows that. How can you have friends if you never see anyone?'

'I s-see people. My family and ... our ward–' Retra stopped. She'd said too much.

'Warden? You have a warden visit? What did you do wrong?'

Retra dropped her head. The warden had been sent to watch her family after Joel left, but she didn't want to tell Cal that – or anything else.

'Yeah, well, family still amounts to nothing.' Cal stood up. She wasn't very tall, and her white hair fell almost to her waist. In Grave North the girls had to wear their hair bound but Cal had untied hers already. It made Retra feel self-conscious.

She watched the girl walk off along the deck until she reached the barge's large cabin housing, where she disappeared from sight.

The murmur of voices drifted back to Retra from the same direction. The other runaways would be down there. Perhaps she should join them; there might be food and something to drink. Her last meal had been well over a day ago. Mother had served braised livers with kumara and snake beans. The same meal they'd had the night Joel ran away; the night they'd been put on probation; the night the warden had stapled the obedience patch to Retra's thigh. Then he'd placed electro-eyes around the house so he could watch her family eat and dress and other private things.

Father had born the intrusion like penance. Mother scarcely seemed to notice, consumed by her sadness. But Retra hated it. She took to dressing in the shower cubicle while she was still wet, and shivering through the morning in damp clothes.

Now hunger pains clawed at her stomach, snapping her back to the present. She uncramped her legs and forced herself upright. She'd starved herself after her last meal, keeping the hunger at bay with cranberry juice.

Pain can make you vomit. Best handled on an empty stomach. Joel had said that too.

But she should eat now, before the weakness became too great. Yet she was afraid. Was the food safe to eat? What if the others on the barge were like Cal? What if they despised Seals? She wasn't used to groups of people. In the Seal compound, people her age were forbidden to gather together.

That hadn't mattered really. Not while Retra had Joel. But when he'd left, the loneliness had gnawed at her like weevils at dry bones. That's when she'd started to practise enduring physical pain. It distracted her from the hurt inside. Now that she was on her way to Ixion, though, the inside hurt had become a hollow fear.

Gripping the handrail, she let it guide her towards the cabin. Counting steps calmed her.

There were 1592 steps from her parents' front door, across the grey cobblestones of the main courtyard, along the separate walking paths, to the fence of the Seal compound. She'd counted them many times in her head; pushing aside her sadness by filling her mind with the numbers. The compound gate was locked, opened only on Sundays when the Grave traders brought in groceries.

The obedience strip began to glow at 1492 steps, and with it came the pain. A hundred steps before the fence. Stabbing then easing, then stabbing harder. Like a branding iron sizzling skin at first touch, then easing in a rush of endorphins, only to turn into an inescapable agony as it bit deeper into the skin.

Retra knew how branding felt. Seal girls and boys received theirs at puberty. The strong ones didn't make a sound when the hot iron bit their flesh. Retra hadn't been strong. Then.

Twenty-five, twenty-six, twenty-seven … The pain had eased but now she needed to count for calm.

When she reached the cabin she slowed. *Fifty. Fifty-one.* Past the corner of the housing. A glimpse of stairs. Then she saw the barge's wide, flat stern, lit by glowing balls that dangled above a trestle table from invisible threads.

Some of the runaways were gathered around the table and the scraps left on the stainless steel food platters. The rest were huddled in groups, sitting on the floor. Cal was on the floor.

Seventy-five. Seventy-six. Retra reached for the crumbs of some cake and a pastry she didn't recognise. The others had already eaten, giving her the confidence to try it.

She slipped the food into the pocket of her coat and began to back away until her hands touched the hard texture of a lifeguard ring hanging on the cabin wall.

Return to the bow, she told herself. But her breath caught in her chest; the Riper was back, standing in front of her. *What does he want?*

Without a word he leaned forward as if he meant to grab her but at the last moment he brushed past her waist, reaching behind her, into the dark hollow behind the ring buoy.

She heard a muffled gasp.

He wrenched backwards fiercely and a body catapulted from the cavity, knocking Retra sideways so that she stumbled over outstretched legs and fell close to Cal.

'No!' pleaded a young woman, grabbing at the buoy. But the Riper tore her loose and dragged her away towards the cabin stairs.

'She must be too old,' said Cal.

Retra picked herself up. She swallowed to ease her dry throat. Fear made her shivery. 'What will happen to her?'

Cal shrugged. She turned her head in the other direction. 'She was stupid to try to come here if she was too old. Everyone knows they don't let you in.'

It sounded callous, but Cal was only pretending not to care. She was scared, Retra could tell, by the way she jiggled her leg and hugged her arms tight to her body.

Seal silence had taught Retra to understand the things people did with their hands and their bodies. She wanted to say something reassuring but couldn't think of the right words. And she wasn't sure if Cal would want it.

Instead, she climbed to her feet and retraced her steps to the bow.

It got colder as the engines propelled them through the waves. Mist stole across the bow and cloaked the barge, so that the dangle of party lights were only a bleary rainbow.

Snatches of conversation drifted down to Retra as she took bites of the strangely flavoured food. It was not unpleasant and it took the edge off the gnawing in her stomach.

'Rules for everything in Grave,' one girl said. 'And the bells. Everything must be done by the bells. I've been waiting since I was twelve to come here.'

Others joined in. None of them spoke of missing home or family, only celebrated their escape from penance and prayers and isolation.

I'm not like them, thought Retra.

She didn't crave parties and fun. All she wanted was to see Joel, and feel safe again. The familiar ache returned to her chest – the one that had driven her from home to find her brother. How long had he been gone? How long, waking up every morning with that heaviness pressing at her heart? Endless, endless days of feeling lost.

Did he cower like me on the bow of this dismal boat?

No. Joel never cowered, not even before her father and the Council of the Seal Enclave. He'd been born with free will in his veins; wanting to read what he wanted, do as he pleased. He'd tried to teach her to be the same but mostly she was too scared. The one time she had, she'd been caught – listening to *the Angel Arias*. Joel had stood up for her against them all. Taken the blame.

Part of her had rejoiced that day; but another part wished he had kept quiet, the way they'd been taught. Keeping quiet meant Father would not have snake-whipped him and he wouldn't have run away and left her alone.

two

A noise woke Retra from a chilled and uneasy doze. Disorientated, she looked around for the source of the disturbance, standing to peer over the side of the barge. The dark sea boiled where it met the boat's underbelly, sending sprays of water up the side. The salt stung her eyes. She clung to the railing, listening to shouts and screams coming from the waterline. Something was wrong.

Suddenly, the party lights extinguished and invisible wings beat in the air above her. She dropped to her knees and crawled back towards the cabin, frightened to stay where she was.

Just before she reached the stairs, the barge juddered as if running into something and she sprawled forward. Her outstretched hands touched flesh. She bit off a cry as a hand grabbed her arm and helped her to sit upright.

'Hey, it's all right,' said a soothing male voice.

She strained to see him. He seemed broad; solid, in the grainy light. Alongside him Retra recognised a smaller figure whose swathe of white hair glowed with light of its own.

'Cal?'

Cal leaned against the guy, their shadows melding into one, and whispered too loudly, 'She's a Seal.'

The guy moved his hand quickly from Retra's arm.

She wanted to tell him that she wasn't contaminated, that she was just the same as him, but the noise around them intensified with urgent shouts and footsteps.

Several Ripers appeared and sped past them, so quickly that Retra heard the clatter of their boots but only glimpsed the flicker of their long coats.

The boy next to her climbed to his feet and peered over the side. Retra and Cal copied him.

A blood-red flare burst across the starboard sky and Retra saw a sleek, stingray-shaped powerboat floating alongside them. Leashed echo-locaters hovered on giant wings above it, screeching.

'How can she harness them like that?' asked Retra. She shivered, picturing how they roamed the night skies of Grave, preying on the smaller of their own kind. Cannibals, Joel had called them.

'It's Ruzalia the pirate,' said the boy. 'She can do anything. She's a body snatcher who steals people for crew. Or because she fancies them.'

'Who told you that?' asked Cal.

'It's in the confetti. They warn you.'

Retra tried to make out his features. 'What do they say?'

'If she raids the barge, stay still. Don't attract attention in case Ruzalia takes you. They say she uses the ones she steals to amuse her. Perform and sing like trained animals.'

'Maybe we should go to the cabin?' Retra began to step away from the draught caused by the beating wings.

'No!' said the boy. His hand shot out and grabbed her wrist. 'Don't! That's where the Ripers took the over-ager. Ruzalia will search everywhere. Especially down there.'

His touch shocked Retra but something about his voice made her feel safer. He had confidence, like Joel. She automatically moved closer to him.

Sensing her reaction, he relaxed his grip. But it tightened again as a body loomed up over the edge of the railing close to them.

Suddenly, the pirates were everywhere. Running along ledges on nimble feet, using swords to flip over piles of rope, and jab behind casings.

Another flare shot skyward, exploding in red fluorescence.

Some of the other Grave runaways fled past them towards the bow, screaming.

The boy drew Retra and Cal down into the shadowy hollow of the barge's curved side.

'Keep quiet,' he said.

They were close enough to the cabin to see a Riper emerge from down below. When the Riper reached the top of the stairs a pirate jumped on him from above. But the Riper shifted, leaving the pirate to crash to the deck. Then the Riper leapt upon him, moving with unnatural speed, dragging him downwards.

Shouts and deep growling noises emanated from below.

'What was that?' Retra whispered.

'Sssh,' said the boy, pointing upwards.

A tall figure straddled the railing immediately above them. Long legs slid over, boots almost scraping Retra's head. The boy reacted quickly, pulling Retra hard against him so that the pirate missed stepping on her.

The booted figure jumped down lightly, sword in hand, and sprinted towards the stairs. Long hair flared out over leather-clad shoulders. One agile leap took her down into the cabin and the growling stopped abruptly.

Retra felt the boy holding his breath; imagined she could hear the thud of his heart. Or maybe that was hers? She was used to fear, but not closeness; her chest on his stomach, his knee resting against her thigh, his breath close enough that she felt its damp warmth.

She began to pull away but he didn't let go.

'Wait! Watch. In case ...' He tapered off.

Retra tilted her head back towards the cabin. What did he mean?

A moment later the tall pirate exploded back up the stairs, half-dragging, half-carrying a limp form – the over-ager, Retra realised. With her free hand she brandished her sword. She retraced her steps, bringing her to the exact spot alongside Retra again.

The boy, Cal and Retra huddled closer as the pirate dropped her sword to lift the body over the railing. The weapon clattered down close to Retra, spattering her with something wet and sticky.

'Catch her,' said the pirate, in a stern and commanding voice to those waiting in the stingray boat below.

'Please, don't hurt me,' begged the scared young woman.

'I'm saving you, if you keep quiet and do as you're told,' said the pirate. She reached down for the hilt of the sword and saw Retra.

Fierce eyes peered at her and the point of the pirate woman's blade flicked up against Retra's temple, lifting her veil.

Retra froze, paralysed by her own terror. Would the pirate kill her? Or take her?

But the pirate frowned with recognition at the veil and let it slip back in place. The boy hauled her away onto his lap, arms sliding around her as if he were protecting a child.

The pirate stared at them both and the moment lasted longer than any Retra had known; longer than when the warden had stapled on her obedience strip.

Then the woman gave a wink and, as suddenly as she'd come, her sword flipped away and she was gone.

'Ruzalia,' breathed the boy. 'Hair redder than fire and her blade as quick.' He laughed, shakily. 'I guess she got what she came for, and that was enough.'

As if the pirate captain had heard him, her sharp voice bellowed from below, 'Ditch this tub!'

Retra slid off the boy's lap and sprang up to watch. Several pirates leapt from the barge to the water and the cruiser swept around in a tight arc to scoop them up.

'No one can catch Ruzalia. She's too fast,' sighed the boy. He and Cal were standing now as well. 'And smart.' He sounded impressed; envious, perhaps.

'And lucky,' said Cal.

Retra strained to follow the fading wash the stingray boat left behind in the dark as Ruzalia sped away.

Quiet settled on the barge and the party lights came back on. A spotlight began to rove the decks. It revealed groups of the runaways still clinging to each other at the bow. Ripers moved about the deck, urging them back to the stern.

Retra turned to the boy. In the spotlight she saw him properly for the first time and her stomach knotted. Smooth skin and full lips framed by hair that curled around his ears and down onto the collar of his coat. His eyes might be hazel, she thought, or grey, and his deep, soulful look made her eyes sting. She dropped her gaze to her feet in case he thought she was tearful.

'Thank you f-for ...' She tapered off.

'I'm Markes. From Grave North.' He thrust his hand into her blurred vision.

'Retra, from Seal South.' She heard the apology in her own voice.

'I've heard that the Ripers don't like Seals. You might want to change your name,' he warned her softly. 'As it is, you were lucky Ruzalia didn't take you. She knows everyone who comes on. No one knows how. But she does.'

The thought of it started Retra trembling. What she had done to see Joel again – the pain. If the pirate had taken her ... 'Why does she do that?'

Markes shrugged. 'It's hard to know the truth. Some say it's a rescue. Others say she's perverted and cruel and uses them as pets. The truth may be somewhere in between.'

'Whatever.' Cal tugged at Markes's arm until he faced her. 'The over-ager deserved it. You can't come to Ixion when you're old.'

The spotlight showed that Cal's white hair framed a heart-shaped face, made prettier by upturned lips and long-lashed blue eyes. She was attractive in a way that Retra immediately envied.

Not that Retra had much to compare with – the women in the Seal compound wore veils, and the men wore deep-caps that hid the sides of their faces. But Cal was beautiful.

'She shouldn't be pretending she's young enough for Ixion,' continued Cal. 'She had her chance to come here when she was younger. It's our place. Our time.'

'We all pretend things sometimes. And sometimes we leave things too late.' Markes showed his disagreement with her by turning back to Retra.

He reached out and wiped his finger across Retra's cheek. 'There's blood on you from Ruzalia's blade. You never made a sound when she pointed it at you.'

Retra trembled, not knowing what to do with the admiration in his voice, or her body's reaction to his touch. She wasn't going to Ixion for the same reason as Cal – for parties and boys. She wanted only to find her brother.

I can't live like this anymore, Ret, Joel had told her. *I'm suffocating*.

Her brother had been all impulse and quick, blazing heat. She'd felt so cold without him. But right now, Markes's touch and his gentle, steady gaze warmed her.

'Yeah, you're covered in it. You should go and clean up, you look terrible,' said Cal. 'We'll be in Ixion soon.'

In the silence that fell between them, the engines seemed to throb louder than before, straining to get there.

Retra bit her tongue and frowned. Cal wanted to be left alone with Markes – that was obvious. She risked a glance and found that he was staring intently at her. He didn't speak, though, or offer to come with her.

Under Markes's silent scrutiny and Cal's disapproval, she fumbled for the handrail, and made her way aft looking for somewhere to wash.

The barge's ablution cubicle was on the far side of the cabin housing. Retra waited her turn in line, head bowed to conceal the blood on her face. She listened to the conversations around her, about Ruzalia and Ixion. Some sounded excited, others scared.

'I've heard Ruzalia ran away to Ixion and didn't like it. So she started stealing people to make her own place –'

'That's stupid. How could you not like Ixion? Ixion is freedom.'

'Did you see her boat? And the giant bat things –'

'She killed a Riper. They put his body in the kitchen. I saw them drag it –'

'It's everywhere, all over the walls.'

Retra touched her face. Was it Riper's blood? She felt sick.

The toilet cubicle became free and she stumbled into it. There was no lock, so she jammed her heel against the door. With jerky movements she removed her veil and splashed her face, heedless of the ice cold water. There was no mirror but Retra didn't need it. She'd practised washing and dressing all her life without one. Seals believed mirrors bred vanity.

With fingers well accustomed to the contours of her face, she checked for cleanliness across her brow and cheekbones, then down to the fading scar on her earlobe, where the warden had stung her with the pain prodder for asking to go to the library.

The prodder hadn't been as bad as the obedience strip, though. When the warden fitted the strip, he'd pored over her naked thigh for ages, pressing and prodding the soft skin there; pushing her underwear aside to make sure it wouldn't interfere with the proper function.

Her embarrassment had been so intense she'd wanted to shrivel into nothing. And the warden had tested it for days, at any time, making sure it triggered pain-shocks whenever he chose. Sometimes he woke her in the night with it; sometimes he activated it during dinner. One time, the pain made her sick up her meat soup, and Father had sent her to her room with nothing more to eat. She hadn't cared by then. Hadn't even cried.

Enduring pain meant practice.

Practice meant escape.

Retra finished the exploration of her face and wiped her skin dry, on the sleeve of her coat. Although her hair was still pinned, she could feel that tendrils had strayed. She let it loose and raked her fingers through it. Joel had thought it a stupid Seal rule – girls and women having to keep their hair tied and covered. *Why have it at all*, he'd say, *if you must keep it hidden*.

Disrespect seemed so easy for him. Retra found it hard, like loving someone who was cruel to you. Cruelty didn't stop you feeling like you belonged. Retra had felt safe in the Seal compound.

Until Joel had gone.

She wound her hair up again, reattached her veil and shifted her heel from the door. She'd return to the bow of

the barge, and sat there, away from Cal and Markes. In the quiet she'd be able to think and plan.

The Riper came for her at dawn. She'd been drowsing, unable to really sleep for the chill, and he'd jerked her from awake with shrill words.

'Come below. Now.'

Cal had been admiring of him earlier, but Retra couldn't see anything appealing in the empty eyes, and the lifeless-cold hands that pulled her to her feet. She noticed a tear in his leather coat and, underneath, a glimpse of something not quite flesh.

It started her trembling again. She snatched her arm back and stabbed her nails into her palms to calm her fear.

'We pass through the edge of the Spiral soon,' he said. 'It won't be safe atop.'

Retra followed him along the deck through the pink fingers of early light that reached as far as the narrow steel steps. As she descended into the cabin, she saw streaks of dark blood smeared the wall, as if someone had missed them while cleaning it in haste.

At the bottom, though, warmth and the buzz of conversation enveloped her. The cabin was brightly lit and crowded with nervous, blinking, talkative Grave runaways. For a moment their anticipation lifted her heavy mood.

She found herself searching for Markes. He leaned against the bulkhead, Cal hanging at his arm, their earlier differences already forgotten.

Retra moved to the opposite side of the cabin, away from them, but Markes caught her eyes and smiled.

Then a Riper began pounding on a drum. Other Ripers descended the steps and spread among the crowd. The tallest ones stooped by the low ceiling, all wearing the same blank stares.

'Sit, all of you,' said one of them. 'The Spiral is not a thing to stand through. You will be perfectly safe from hyper-reaction as long as you stay seated.'

The cabin crowd dropped to the floor in one mass, laughing and falling on each other. Retra squeezed herself into a small space against one wall, trying not to touch the people around her. She wasn't used to crowds; the smell of their bodies made her feel sick.

'What's hyper-reaction?' she heard someone ask.

'It happens when you cross the Spiral. Some get blissed out or real down. But it lasts ... like forever,' answered the girl on one side of her. 'Some even get it afterwards.'

The Riper started speaking again. 'Once through the Spiral, you'll leave the barge and pass into the Register. There you'll be fitted with your badge. After that your life – your pleasure – is your own. *Burn bright!*' The Riper's eyes glittered with strange comprehensions.

'*Burn bright!*' the crowd shouted in enthusiastic response.

Retra glanced to the small, high windows, seeking the sunrise. How long until she saw it again? She suddenly felt thirsty for daylight.

But the hum came.

The cabin lights snuffed out and the barge rocked, gently at first, then wildly – jarring her spine, throwing a boy onto her lap. His red curls brushed against her throat and he cheekily burrowed his freckled face between her breasts. With the roll of the barge he fell backwards again before she could react.

She hugged her knees for protection as the air got thick and heavy and the dawn turned abruptly back to dark. The crowd's eagerness shifted to something fearful.

'What's happening?' shouted one.

Another. 'We're sinking!'

'Fross!'

Huddled in the pitch-black, fear-stink of the cabin, the cries unnerved her. She shut her eyes. *Joel*. She chanted to herself. *Joel*. Saying his name made her feel safer.

Heaviness came next, as if gravity had altered. Breathing got hard. The fear-shouts dwindled.

Then the pain from her obedience strip returned, worse than before. An obscene, tearing hurt that burned from her thigh up to her vertebrae and into her chest. She curled into a ball, biting her tongue to stop from screaming, gouging the flesh of her upper arms with her nails.

Her mind became all; a giant slug filled with ugly, crawling creatures and bad places. And ... noise ... music, she guessed ... but not like anything she had ever heard before.

She pressed her hands to her ears to shut out the raw, thick pulse of it. It stripped her mind of everything and lodged in her belly, churning and quivering. It made her *want* the boy to put his face back between her breasts. She pressed her nipples to stem the sensation. She couldn't bear the wildness of her thoughts.

Then, abruptly, the pain dulled and the music quieted. The barge steadied to a gentle roll and the cabin lit. Retra's eyes flew open, released from the transition. The Riper stood, poised amongst the scatter of bodies, his pale face raised in ecstasy.

'Welcome to Ixion.'

three

They filed from the barge, winter refugees in boots and coats, into an unnatural, sticky heat. Music spread across the surface of the night air like spilled oil, and the flitting shapes of thousands of bats partly obliterated the stars. Retra watched them pour above the barge like a black rainbow across a dark canvas.

So many. Their moist, musky scent assaulted Retra's senses. Between her legs and under her arms became damp with perspiration.

'Look forward,' said a cold voice.

Retra pulled her gaze from the sky to the Ripers. They were watching everyone walk down the drawbridge as if memorising faces. The one who had hauled Retra aboard the barge gave her a mock bow as she shuffled past. She shrank from him, not wanting to be remembered.

The bridge led straight to the back of a large, plain building. Retra tried to see beyond it but bright spotlights along the bridge confused her vision.

Ahead of her in the queue stood Markes and Cal. He had a bulky case slung across his shoulders, an instrument of some kind. Retra wondered if he'd stolen it. In the Seal compound, only Elders were allowed to own such things. Perhaps it was different in Grave North.

The pair was nearly at the Register. She wanted to get closer to Markes – just to say good luck, she told herself – but that meant speaking to Cal as well, and the girl's manner made her uncomfortable.

Instead, she stopped at the foot of the bridge, suddenly not wishing to leave the barge. Something from out in the dark brushed her throat, damp fingers smearing her with warm wetness. She started, raising a hand against it, but touched nothing.

A teasing whisper in her ear – no, more a thought. *Come to me ...*

She glanced around to see if anyone else had heard, but those near her gazed eagerly ahead. Except the Riper; he watched her.

She bowed her head and hurried on.

The queue split into three lines, each siphoning into a closed booth. She found herself in the line next to Markes just as he disappeared into one with Cal.

At the same time a hand tugged at her shoulder. 'Want to do the same as them?'

It was the boy who'd fallen against her in the Ixion crossover. She recognised his freckled skin and the way his red curls corkscrewed off in different directions. Now that he was standing, she could see that he was taller than her but not nearly as big as Markes. She blushed, remembering her thoughts during the transition.

'Hey, I know you! You've got soft whatsies.' He leered at her chest, unashamed. 'I'm Rollo. Looks like you can go through the Register in pairs. Wanna do that?'

Retra shook her head.

His leer deflated. 'Hey, I didn't think girls came here to give knock-backs.'

She turned away, offended. Maybe Cal was right about Seals. She hadn't talked to any boys, other than Joel. Seal boys and girls were always chaperoned. Crossing her arms tight across her chest, she ignored Rollo's fake heavy breathing down her neck.

Jerk! A forbidden word but it felt good to say it in her mind.

Rollo's teasing stopped abruptly, though, when the boy who'd gone into the booth before them burst back out, moaning and crying. He threw himself to the ground near her feet, tearing at his face with his fingers, trying to gouge his own eyes out.

Two Ripers appeared and carried him away.

Hyper-reaction, the whisper went round.

Dread wound around Retra's stomach. *Will that happen to me?*

She forced herself to step into the vacant booth. It was empty other than a black circle painted on the floor and an articulated metallic arm that hung from the ceiling.

As she stepped into the circle the door closed behind her and the mechanical arm dropped down, a hand of instruments unfolding from it. A brace snapped tight around her head and probes skittered into her ears and nose. She felt pinpricks at the base of her spine and neck.

Biological age 6387 days. Health – acceptable. Adrenal modifications successful. Psychological/neurological profile recommends faux badge. Proceed. Place your hand between the plates, said a disembodied voice.

She complied with the voice and the plates closed together, locking her hand in position. A probe punctured the skin at the centre of her palm, making her twist in pain.

Faux badge administered. Test orientation download … starting … now …

After the blackness passed, she woke up on the floor in another bare room. She was alone in it, apart from Markes. He leaned against the wall, hands in his coat pockets, hair curling over his eyes, watching her.

Her tunic had ridden high up her thighs. Embarrassed, she smoothed it down. She wanted to move closer to him, as if proximity might ease the dull throb in her thigh and the sharper, newer, sickening pain in the palm of one hand.

She rose up onto her elbows. *Better not*. The last thing she wanted was to be sick on Markes.

He came to her instead, kneeling, grasping her shoulders, giving them a little shake.

'How are you?' he asked.

'W-what happened to me?'

'The probes give some people grief.' He shrugged his hair from his eyes long enough for her to get a shiver from their liquid warmth. Then he moved his face closer, as if he might put his cheek to hers. 'Why do I get the feeling you're here for a different reason than the rest of us?'

Retra turned her head away from his. His closeness suffocated and elated her; stirred things in her.

'They put something on my hand. Th-then they tested it and … I woke up in here with you,' she said.

His fingers tightened, crushing her shoulder bones. His lips hovered near her earlobe, breath so light she could barely ... No! She *couldn't* feel it.

He persisted with his question. 'Why are you here?'

'I –' Her desire to tell him the truth compelled her to speak, as if confession might absolve her of guilt and the fear, but a sliver of suspicion pierced her consciousness as she opened her mouth.

No breath. He has no breath.

The pain in the palm of her hand snaked up her arm to her skull and stung the bridge of her nose. But Retra knew pain. Knew how to think through it.

'I-I want to have a good time, that's all,' she stammered.

She reached a hand out to his lips, to test their moistness, but Markes and the room dissolved before her eyes. A heartbeat later the pain stopped and the Register released her from the cubicle into the dark.

She stumbled out of the exit, dazed, and was caught by the chill hands of a Riper – the same one who'd pulled her aboard the barge and then watched her leave it. She found herself unable to struggle, as he carried her from the Register to a narrow path strewn with rock and encroached upon by the undergrowth of the darker dark. He knelt, laying her onto the ground.

She had a vague impression of movement in the twilight to the side of them.

Smell good, said the invisible voice/thought again.

The Riper made a hissing noise. He leaned over her, his hair falling across her face, filling her vision with his ashen skin and hollow eyes. 'The Register is satisfied but I am not. I'll be watching you. You remind me of someone,' he said.

His touch triggered a bottomless fear in her. When one long, pale finger looped a strand of her hair, she lapsed into shivers.

'W-what d-do you m-mean?'

He lifted the strand to his mouth and slid it between his lips as if tasting it.

Growling, unearthly noises crawled into the air around them and the Riper let go of the strand.

Mine, said the thought/voice.

The Riper stiffened and backed away from her then he vanished into the dark.

Retra lay trembling. As her body began to calm, nausea claimed her and she rolled on her side and vomited.

'Is someone over there?' called a voice.

'Here,' she managed.

Rollo stood on the edge of the lit area, squinting over to where she lay. 'It's you. What happened? You're s'posed to stay on the main paths.'

He walked over to her and bent awkwardly to avoid stepping off the path.

Grateful, and ashamed at her earlier opinion of him, she reached out and took his hand.

'The Register ... made me sick,' she said. 'I wandered a bit, without meaning to.'

'Lucky I heard you. You could have gotten lost.'

He pulled her up and helped her back to the wide, well-lit path, considerately not mentioning the sour vomit smell about her.

'You all right?'

She nodded, straining away from his contact, now that she was upright and the dizziness had passed.

He didn't seem to notice her discomfort. 'Wow, would you look at that!' He pointed ahead.

Retra glanced up. Despite her nervousness a thrill pimpled her skin as she absorbed and made sense of the view: lights of every colour, some in soaring arcs, some in clusters, others scattered – ruby, glowing cobalt and bullion gold. A streak of emerald snaked through the middle, dividing the vista in two. The light haloes bled into each other, forming misty night rainbows.

'Are they dirigibles?' she asked, uncomprehending. 'Or levia-flies? I've heard they come this way.'

He laughed. 'Those are the clubs. Set into the cliffs.' He whistled in awe. 'Must be some big crater.'

She turned back to him for an explanation.

He stuck out his chest as if pleased that he knew more than her. 'The island is the tip of a volcano. Came up out the sea one day. That was a long time ago, even before the Elders came to Grave.'

'The Elders wanted to start again and build a better society so they left the Old Place,' she said, automatically. 'The Old Place had no rules and Technology was an evil God.'

'Maybe,' said Rollo. 'If you believe our history lessons.'

Retra stared at him, astonished. 'Don't you believe them?'

Rollo shrugged. 'It's one version of things.'

'What do you mean?'

'Well, take this place. Some say that when it rose up out of the sea, people thought it was a holy place. That's when there was still day and night. Monks from different provinces came here and built churches. They tried to outdo each other and impress God. God didn't like what they were doing so he took the light away.'

Retra kept quiet, not wanting to interrupt the story by asking him what a province was, or how he knew these things.

'Another version reckons that all the nearby provinces wanted to claim Ixion as their own land, so they fought over it. Every time one of them won a battle they built their own holy place. Then someone would come and fight them for it, take it and build another church. They say there was so much death that the colour leached out of the sky.'

'Can that happen?' Retra didn't think so, but the stories entranced her.

'Dunno. Sounds pretty stupid to me. Whatever happened, the monks that lived in the churches vanished.'

'How could they vanish?'

'Maybe demons got them.' He pulled a horrible face at her and she wanted to scold him for his silliness.

'Don't make light of such things,' she said.

'You Seals take stuff too serious.'

'How did you know I was a Seal?'

'Easy. Seals don't get taught anything much. Your Elders think it's dangerous and the Council likes it that way too. Plus you've got that look. The way you look down all the time. The girls in Grave North aren't so timid and they look at you when they speak.' He held out his palm and drew invisible lines on it. 'Ixion's like this. The barge comes in on the low, submerged side of the crater and the clubs are built up and down the cliffs of the higher side.'

'How do you get up there to them?'

He grabbed her hand. 'Dunno. But let's find out.'

four

They walked slowly, overtaken by others coming through the Register. Some ran, unable to contain their excitement.

Retra felt the lure of the night rainbows just as surely as she'd felt the hidden beast lurking at the side of the path. She found herself stepping carefully, delicately, between the warring forces of beauty and danger. The rainbows caused a shiver of anticipation to run across her flesh. But at the same time she was drawn to the shadows beyond the path, the sounds of scraping and the scent of perfumed rot.

'What's wrong with you?' Rollo asked.

'The Ripers. They scare me a little.'

He laughed. 'Crowd control. They're meant to. It's just mental intimidation.'

'Do you think so?'

But Rollo wasn't listening to her. 'Look, here's your answer. That explains the strip down the middle.'

Ahead of them an ancient cable kar, gleaming with ornate dark-metallic trim and ingrained wood panelling hung adjacent to a paved station platform. The kar was attached to a glowing emerald cable that stretched away into the night, up the side of the crater.

A bell began to toll ponderously.

'Come on,' called someone. 'This kar's leaving in a moment.'

'Quick!' Rollo pulled her on board when she would have hesitated. The doors closed and everyone crammed together to look out of the open windows, shouting into the dark in excitement.

Retra wanted to shut their noise out, desperately wanted their silence, but all she could do was press her hands to ears.

'What's wrong?' Rollo tried to tear her hands away.

She shook him off and prayed.

Silence is my duty,

Calm my reward.

She repeated the Seal mantra over and over as protection from the noisy jubilation. Only when the cable kar stopped did she open her eyes.

It hung next to an elevated platform from which stairs disappeared down into the dark. A slender girl dressed in a long, velvet dress cut away to show her stomach and the low curve of her breasts stepped from the shadows, as if she'd been waiting. The strings of her bodice trailed onto the ground. Around her, a drumbeat sounded. She beckoned to them with a shrill whisper. 'Critical Zone, babies. I dare you.'

Two boys, the noisiest ones, jumped out from the kar windows, stumbling over each other, laughing, punching each other's arms.

The girl smiled at them in a way that constricted Retra's heart. It was as though the girl was a hunter revelling at the sight of weak prey.

'Idiots,' observed Rollo. 'Zoners don't get to go anywhere else.'

Retra looked at him blankly.

'You never read the confetti?'

She shook her head, not wanting to explain about her father's punishments.

'Zoners aren't allowed to use the churches. So they don't get to rest, ever.' He was doing his best not to look frightened.

'What does that mean for them?' she whispered, watching the backwash of shadows close behind them as the kar rumbled on.

'I think that means they don't last as long.' He held up his palm and Retra saw the small tattoo in the centre of it. 'The badge implant they gave us at the Register reduces our need to sleep but we still have to rest sometimes. Zoners can't do that. It's the one rule of their club. Burn bright and burn out – real quick!'

Retra was staring at him now, wide eyed. She slowly turned her hand over. Her tattoo was different to Rollo's; duller and less defined, as though it hadn't been properly administered. She quickly closed her fist. 'That must be awful. Why would you go there?'

'Dunno,' he shrugged. 'The girl behind me at the Register said everything's better there. Sharper. More intense.' He grabbed Retra's hands and raised them up in the air so they swayed together like everyone else in the car. 'I prefer to take it a bit slower. We're gonna have fun. Let's party!'

Retra snatched her hands back and turned away from him, pressing against the metallic window trim as the kar carried them higher into the night.

She became mesmerised by the brilliant streamers of lights, using them as a distraction from the raw mix of drums and synthesisers pumping through the speakers.

The kar rocked to the rhythm of the wires above and shook with the shuffling of feet. Bodies banged into her the way they had on the barge. She gripped the cooler metal of the window until it bruised her fingers, and prayed for the trip to end.

Moist, warm air slid over her, mocking her heavy coat and thick socks. Around her some of the others began to shed their clothing like skins of moulting reptiles. They dropped them at their feet, stamping and yelling.

Next to her, Rollo tore his coat off and unbuttoned his shirt. Beneath it his belly gleamed, white and dimpling soft. The sight of his flesh made her queasy.

'Put it back on,' she whispered. 'Please.'

But he didn't hear her. He leaned close to a girl with tight curls, talking. *No. Not talking. Kissing.* Retra's pulse raced at the idea and her queasiness intensified.

Rollo nuzzled at the girl's neck, ignoring Retra until the kar arrived at another dimly lit, already crowded platform.

Everyone tried to leave at once. Retra stumbled, knocking her knee against a pole as she stepped down. She straightened, catching a glimpse of Markes again – then he was gone.

Rollo appeared beside her and grabbed her hand. 'Why didn't you wait for me?' he asked.

She scowled at him. 'Why were you doing *that* with a stranger?'

'Not a stranger, her name is Keltha and she kisses like a devil.' He poked out his tongue and rolled it around obscenely.

Retra pulled her hand from his. His baiting and his crudeness stung.

Seeing her reaction, his expression grew serious for a moment. 'Get over it, Retra. You have to fit in here. It's the only way.'

She stared at him, not quite sure what he meant. Then the crowds began to surge forward down the stairs and into a vast, lit empty space.

Retra clung to the gates at the top, looking down at the huge stone columns on one side which seemed to be carved out of the mountain. On the far side, ornate ironwork rails marked the edge of a steep, dark precipice. Between the railing and the columns, in the centre of the field, fire jets spurted into the sky, spreading jagged light across a burgundy velvet-cloaked stage.

Rollo tugged at her again. 'Come on, we won't be able to hear if we stay here.'

She followed him down the steps, her irritation with him banished by wonder. She'd never seen so many people in one place.

Rollo forced a path for them, determinedly elbowing his way between the excited crush of bodies to the front. Retra saw six figures standing at different points of the stage, all motionless in the flickering light of the fire spouts.

'Silence.' A single word, issued from the person at the centre. It echoed more than it should have, sibilant and eerie, quieting the crowd. It caught in her mind.

'I am Lenoir, leader of the Guardians. This may be the only time we will meet, so listen well. What you fail to hear becomes your lot to bear.'

He waited then, letting his words impact.

Retra stood as still as him, transfixed by his manner and look; the lustre of the black hair that framed his pale, flawless face. He was beautiful in a way Retra had never seen before.

Unholy.

A Seal mantra moved her lips but she clamped them together. Now was not the time for her Grave ways. She must listen and learn or ... *God*. Another unbidden thought. *He is like God.*

But what did she know of God? What did she know of men?

And yet the drift of his long hair and his worldly sneer made her stomach clench with unwanted emotion.

'I – we ...' he gestured dramatically, left and right, 'own you now. This is our place.'

The silence became taut as if the crowd breathed in accord.

Lenoir laughed, feeling it. Though many could not see him as well as she could, he mesmerised them with his voice alone.

'Fear not. All we want ... is for you to pleasure yourselves,' he said.

A cheer went up, discharging the tension.

He waved his hands once more for quiet. 'In Ixion music and party are our only beliefs. Darkness is our comfort. We have few rules but they are absolute. Your endocrine systems have been altered by changes to your hypothalamus. You no longer need to sleep or see sunlight.'

More titters and cheers. A little frayed and scared, Retra thought.

'Still, you will need to rest for a short period every twelve-cycle; how long will vary for each of you. When that time is upon you, the badge you have had administered at the Register will glow. We call this rest *petite nuit* – little night.' He laughed, 'Your body needs to rest and yet your mind will remain conscious. That is the time for you to be in your beds, little ones. If you ignore this, it is at your own risk.'

Catcalls and whistles followed this.

Retra watched a smile catch and linger on his lips as if he enjoyed an amusing secret.

A young woman moved from one side of the stage to join him. Her naked scalp glowed in the amber light, yet she was not quite bald; dark hair sprang from the edge of her skull like a collar of spikes. In profile her nose was perfectly straight, her lips thin. She wore hard leather on her arms and legs, and a shaped tunic.

Retra's stomach fluttered. In Grave, woman wore veils and heavy, shapeless gowns. They kept their eyes downcast and spoke softly.

'My name is Test, baby bats. Listen well. The mountain is strewn with paths that connect Ixion's clubs. They are well lit and safe enough. Should you venture off them and into the dark, you will not return. Remember, when you live in a place of darkness you also live with creatures of the dark.'

Test's slow, husky voice might have been just next to Retra's ear, caressing her with a warning.

'How do they do that?' whispered Rollo. 'It's like she's in my head.'

Retra ignored him, straining forward.

A few cocky ones in the crowd gave catcalls.

Lenoir stared them back into silence.

'The Guardians –' the woman continued.

'Ripers,' Rollo hissed in Retra's ear.

'– are here for your guidance and protection. Ask us anything but heed our advice. We dispense our justice. Respect us. Do not attempt to ... *be* with us. We are apart.'

This time the catcalls were cacophonous.

Test reached for Lenoir's hand; pale exotic creatures united.

Lenoir spoke again. 'Ixion has six churches on consecrated ground: Vank, Illi, Agios, Goa and Los Fien. That is where you may slumber safely and gain sustenance. There is only one church you are not permitted to enter: Danskoi on the highest tier is our domain. If you enter you will not return.'

The other Ripers gathered around Lenoir and Test. Retra tried to memorise their faces.

Test spoke again. 'Now only the cleansing ceremony remains before you can begin again. Drink Lava from the dispensing stations then remove your clothes and bring them to the pyres.'

She gestured to the pyramids of brush in front of the railings that safeguarded the crowd from the precipice.

For a moment nobody moved then Ripers began to walk amongst them, snatching at hats and tossing them in the air, tugging at the coats of those still clinging to Grave memories.

Rollo stripped his long pants off. Underneath he wore nothing.

Retra recoiled from his dangling nakedness, her chest banging her ribs hard with shock, but around her others began to do the same.

She became caught in the melee as they grabbed cups of Lava and surged towards the pyres. The drink seemed to heighten their fervour, and their hot flesh brushed against her.

A female Riper with waist-length streaks of black and white hair and raised scars along her hairline appeared alongside Retra and wrenched at her veil and coat. The veil fluttered to the ground like an injured moth and the grey wool tunic caught, twisted and tore where it was most worn.

With eager hands the Riper pulled it apart like a curtain.

Retra screamed at the violation but the Riper was already tossing her clothes high onto the piles of branches along with the others.

Rollo danced off to join the milling, naked bodies gathering like children eager for a bonfire, leaving Retra huddled on the ground trying to cover her skin with her arms.

'You need cleansing, dirty little bat.' The scarred Riper pushed something into her hand. 'Drink this. It will stir your blood.'

As Retra put the cup to her mouth, the Riper bent to unhook the remains of her tunic and push it from her shoulders. The garment slid down and she smeared a warm sticky substance over Retra's back.

The scarred woman's touch panicked her beyond sense. She pulled away from her and ran, zigzagging through the crowd. Everyone was screaming and singing and pushing in the opposite direction.

Retra tried to remember Test's words. *Ixion has six churches on consecrated ground. Vank, Illi, Agios ... you may slumber safely and gain sustenance.*

Dressed only in her underwear, she stumbled up the stairs. A cable kar waited there, swaying gently. She ran into the first carriage and banged the speaker. 'Take me to a church.'

Nothing happened and she feared that the shouts and clamour near the base of the stairs meant the crowd had followed her.

She picked a name she could remember from the Riper's list. 'Vank. Take me to Vank.'

The kar groaned and moved forward, gradually picking up momentum.

Cries of 'wait for us' and 'come back' trailed after her in the dark. She shrank from them as she had from the prying fingers of the Riper, huddling into the hard leather of the seat.

'There'll be others.' A last shout faded.

The kar transported her higher, clunking through an interchange before arcing onto a subsidiary line.

Retra peered through the window, wondering why daylight never came here. Joel had talked of Ixion but she had not really listened, not really believed he would go there. Every season Grave North lost some of their youth to the lure of the Dark Island – but not Seal South.

Seals knew better than to look for pleasure.

The kar slowed to a halt at a station where a sign wavered under a light so fragile that it seemed as if one more rumble from the carriage might extinguish it forever.

'Vank station. This kar will leave in ten tolls,' said the speaker-voice.

Hugging herself, she stepped out onto the platform. At the foot of the long stairs she saw another platform that served as a terrace to the entry of a huge stone church.

She glanced around as she descended; either end of the terrace disappeared into darkness, and the edges drew her in the same way a precipice held fascination to those fearful of heights.

She left the stairs and crept to one end to peer into the darkness. The drop was steep and dangerous. Shapes appeared from the darkness below, blurred at first then becoming solid. Her father's face, bloated with anger, hovering atop the body of a blood-slicked, glistening demon. Long, cruel nails grasped for her.

You have disgraced us!

Jamming fingers in her mouth to stop a scream, she ran to the bolted doors and tugged at the bell. When no one answered she banged at the door, trembling and sobbing.

Finally a girl appeared, holding a flickering candle.

'You are early. Welcome to the Church of Vank. Hush now, baby bat, never stray from the paths and know when you must rest. I am Charlonge.'

Retra clasped her hands together, prayer-like. 'Please … I need clothes.'

Charlonge frowned at the underwear for a moment before she slipped her arm around Retra. 'Of course you do. You all do at the beginning. Come.'

As they entered the church, Retra barely registered the marble alcoves with their candlelit miniature statues, or the vases of satin-black flowers. She spent her energy on walking, and on listening to Charlonge's gentle instructions.

'Up there behind the praying pews. That's right. We have beds awaiting our new baby bats. Soon you can rest. Up the stairs, little one.'

Retra recoiled against the balustrade.

'What hurts ye?' asked Charlonge.

'N-nothing hurts,' Retra gasped. 'But I-I'm almost n-naked, I c-cannot be seen by others.'

Charlonge's solicitous expression tightened. She pulled Retra to her feet and seized her shoulders. 'I'll say this one time only. Don't show your fears and weaknesses. In this place they'll devour you as sure as the night.' She bent her face close, her breath sweet but her tone as sharp as a slap in the face. 'In Ixion, modesty is kin to sin.'

'Who comes, Charlonge?' A Riper appeared at the top of the stairs, pale hair flowing to his shoulders, skin like milk. Retra felt the stillness of the air around him. She forced herself straighter.

'A baby bat that strayed from re-birth, Forlorn,' said Charlonge. 'She lost her way before her clothes could be burned.'

The Riper peered down at them both, hollow-eyed and untrusting. 'See to it.'

'Yes, Forlorn. Of course.'

He glided from their sight down a darkened corridor.

Charlonge gave Retra a hard look. 'Remember why you came here. Seek enjoyment or they will age you quicker.'

Retra nodded. She must learn quickly.

five

Retra lay in a narrow bed. The pearly blue satin of her new sleeping dress felt sinful against her body, and the stiff, white lace of her underwear grazed the soft parts of her flesh as if a deliberate reminder of its decadence.

Charlonge had laid it out for her before leaving. 'Wear this,' she said. She'd also given her a small, numbered key on a thin gold chain. 'Each resting place will have a locker that will match your key. Each locker will have clothes for you. You will always find your locker located in the same room in each of the churches. There are many rooms, don't forget that yours will be in the narthex, close to the front entry.'

'How do they get there? The clothes, I mean.'

'The Ripers choose them for us and the uthers will place them there.'

'Who are the uthers?'

'They are servants of the Guardians. They do the menial work, provide the food and attend the clothes.'

'What do they look like?'

Charlonge frowned. 'It's hard to describe uthers. The live in the corner of your sight. It is easy to overlook them.'

'But where do the Ripers get all the food and the clothes? Ixion is so far from everything else. How do they know what will fit me?'

'They know everything about us. When you change, put your clothes in a collector. They will be cleaned and returned to one of your lockers.' Charlonge's mouth curved in satisfaction. 'We are spared the mundane. It is one of Ixion's – Lenoir's – gifts to us. Our sustenance is provided; we have whatever we want as long as we adhere to his rules. They are few but absolute.'

Retra pictured the beautiful, frightening Guardian. 'Why does Lenoir – why do *they* – do this? Make this place for us?' she asked, her tongue loosened by the cool, sweet drink Charlonge had pressed on her.

Charlonge's smile strained. 'It's not our business to ask such questions. They want us to take pleasure. That is all.'

She'd left, and now, as Retra lay listening to the sounds of others being admitted through the church doors, she wondered again why the Ripers chose to indulge their pleasure so much. What was it that Charlonge had said? Their conversation was becoming blurred. Faint. Then gone, as her mind drowsed without sleeping for some hours, trapped in a reverie of waking dreams – about Joel mostly, but other images as well: the wallowing barge, the uneven, moss-wet stone walls of her home and her father's cold expression when he realised she'd run away and gone after her brother.

How he would hate her for it. How shamed he would be.

Two from the same family, the Seal Superiors would say, *tainted with lust and the lure of profligacy*. Seal families would shun her parents for it. None would offer solace.

Retra emerged from her waking dream state with a dull ache in the base of her throat. *Mother, I'm sorry.* She sobbed without noise: a silent, inner weeping.

Then her thoughts came sharply to the new place, the dreaminess passing. She sat up in bed and scrubbed her face with her fingers.

Candlelit bodies lay in the wrought-iron beds around her, drowsing in their satin and lace. Two were awake, whispering to another. They glanced her way but said nothing to her.

Retra left her bed and slipped barefoot from the room.

The sleeping chamber led to a hall and more rooms with doors firmly shut. Candles, melted in bizarre twisted shapes, lit her way. She touched the key on the chain around her neck and stepped softly. First she must find the clothes Charlonge had spoken about.

But when she reached the stairs, strains of music drew her further on, to the other end of the corridor.

Wall-mounted candelabra lit a grand indoor balcony in a blaze that banished shadows to high corners and revealed the muted colours of the many stained-glass windows. High above, vast arches with thick, decorative ribs marked the ceiling. Beneath her lay the sanctuary of the Church of Vank.

Retra gazed down at the largest apse, where a guitarist sat on an altar strumming something sad. Bodies lounged on a row of pews in the nave, listening and talking quietly. On one side a queue formed outside a curtained confessional: young girls mainly, dressed in black lace and silk, like Retra's sleeping dress, though cut low and revealing. Some looked artfully torn, others were backless.

The memory of Charlonge's words jolted Retra: *Modesty is a sin on Ixion.*

'Well, I guess it's only a small island,' said a sharp voice in her ear.

Retra started and looked around. 'Cal?'

The girl she had met on the barge looked different without her Grave tunic. Her long hair barely masked the gape in the neckline of her sleeping dress.

Retra's eyes were drawn to the girl's naked chest. Her face warmed with embarrassment.

Cal saw her reaction. 'Get over it, Seal. No wonder your kind isn't wanted here.'

The girl's open hostility shocked her; made her wish that their paths had not crossed again. Yet she could not stop herself from asking, 'Is Markes here?'

Cal shrugged and stuck out her lower lip. 'How should I know? I lost track of him at the re-birth. What happened to you? Your boyfriend was looking for you.'

'My b-boyfriend?'

'Rollo, he said his name was. Asking everyone if they'd seen you. Got all worried you'd freaked and jumped over the cliff.'

'I ... wanted to see the churches. This one was the closest.'

Cal stared at her, her eyes glittering suspiciously in the candlelight. 'I don't believe you. I think you ran away from the re-birth. Seals can't take their clothes off. They think flesh is sinful.'

In a quick movement Cal tugged at the neckline of her own satin shift, exposing one of her small breasts. Cal's nipple was pale and soft like an exotic deep-sea creature.

Retra bowed her head, sick to her stomach with shame. She had never seen another girl's body so closely, so brazenly.

'Thought so!' Cal sounded triumphant.

As she tried to think of something to say, the smell of funeral roses filled Retra's senses, telling her that another person had joined them.

'Aaah, baby bats, getting to know each other, I see,' said Charlonge.

Cal released her shift and it fell back to its place over her breast. 'How long do we have to put up with that stupid nickname?'

Charlonge stepped closer to them, breathing the sweet floral scent from her mouth. 'Until you have earned a real one.'

Cal's eyes widened for a moment then she gave a brittle laugh and walked back down the corridor.

'Thank you,' said Retra.

Charlonge sighed. 'You of all must learn quickly ... what Ixion name have you chosen? It is customary for the younglings to do so. A fresh start.'

'I don't know,' answered Retra. The question surprised her. Many would think her Seal name unattractive, but it was still hers. She had no wish to change it. She would not lose her identity in this place.

Charlonge saw her reticence and shrugged. 'Naif would be my choice for you – naive – but there's time enough for choosing, I suppose. Come with me and I'll show you your closet and where you may eat.'

'Is Charlonge your adopted name?' asked Retra as she followed the older girl.

'Yes. I grew up to see things: outside what is visible, I mean. But my people disdained the occult. Somehow "Charlonge" seemed right. It means acceptance, you know.'

Retra didn't understand what Charlonge meant. The occult was not revered in Grave, but neither was it disdained. In Grave it was more sinful to be joyous than a practitioner of the Dark Arts. 'Who are your people?'

'The Lidol from Lidol-Push.'

'Another world?' Retra gasped.

This time Charlonge laughed freely. 'You are truly naive. Your real name should be Naif. Not another world, silly batling, another province. Grave is not the only land near Ixion.'

Retra stared at her, embarrassed and amazed. 'How many others are there?'

'Many.' She laughed. 'I've heard a reaction like yours once before. Are you what they call a Seal?'

Retra nodded.

'Aaah. Then your learning has been very narrow. Your Superiors keep things from you. You must keep your ignorance a secret.'

'What is your land like? How does it look? Where do you find it exactly?' asked Retra.

But Charlonge shook her head. 'Maybe I will answer you another time. Or maybe not. Now, though, you must dress for the Early-Eve. Your sleeping attire will never do.'

As they reached the foot of the staircase, the music swelled in soulful strums, each note more beautiful and sadder than the last. It plucked at Retra's senses.

'Charlonge. The music. Who is playing it? I couldn't see properly from the balcony.'

Charlonge paused. 'Aaah, at last, a good sign from you. You are among many to ask me that question. He is like you – a baby bat. But not for long, I think. His name is Markes and he has wings. Brilliant, jewelled wings.'

Markes was here. Cal had lied to her!

Charlonge beckoned Retra across the entry to what must have once been the church's cloak room. It was now filled with rows of drawers and full-length mirrors.

'We call this the *neglegere*. Beyond it is the wash room. Find your closet and choose your Early-Eve clothes. You must eat in the transept, take confession and then leave. Those who linger are noticed,' she said.

'C-can I come back?'

'Of course, when you need to rest, but not before you have been other places. Baby bats love to explore.' She began to turn away.

'Charlonge, I am looking for someone ...'

Charlonge turned slowly back to face her, a half smile hovering on her lips. 'A boy, no doubt.'

'Yes. But not like that. I'm looking for my brother. He and I ... we look similar, though he is taller and came here a while ago. I m-missed him, so I came after him.'

Charlonge's expression became guarded. 'Do you know how many come to Ixion? How many I see? Why would I remember one boy above another?' she said in a harsh whisper.

Retra flushed, stung by the girl's sudden change of tone. 'Can you tell me where to look? Where would I start?' said Retra softly.

'I would not start. Forget your brother.'

Charlonge walked away, leaving Retra standing alone, unsure of what to do.

Her indecision was broken a moment later when four girls pushed past her. Giggling and talking loudly, they sought their lockers and pulled out their new clothes like birds tearing apart an old nest of twigs.

Retra followed them in and sought the drawer numbered on her key. Again she hesitated before opening it.

One of the girls stripped off her sleeping shift and slipped a thin, see-though shawl around her nakedness. 'Shall I go like this?'

The others snickered and tugged at it, one pulling at the fringe while another uncurled a studded belt from her drawer and slapped the girl's buttocks. She screamed and giggled more.

Their behaviour disturbed Retra and she buried her hands in her face.

The girls ignored her, dancing and cavorting.

'What's your new name?'

Retra looked up. Another girl had entered and opened the drawer next to hers. The new girl flicked a straight, thick lock of hair back from her face and stared at Retra with lively, brown almond eyes.

'I don't know,' said Retra. 'I don't want one.'

The girl hesitated, frowning. 'But everyone has a new name. *Everyone.*'

'Retra is my name,' she stubbornly, waiting for the girl to turn away from her for being a Seal, like Cal had.

'Retra.' The girl let it linger over her tongue. 'It's a tight name but it's okay. Maybe you could go for something softer.'

'Like Naif?' said Retra.

'Oh, that's pretty. Mine is going to be Suki.'

Retra forced herself to respond in kind. 'That's pretty too but I think I'll stay with Retra.'

The girl grinned. 'Fair enough. Do you want to come with me to find the food? I'm starving. All that dancing naked last night, well ... it made me hungry.' She glanced at the others with a disparaging eyebrow. 'I'm over it now, though.'

Retra's lips curled involuntarily. Suki's direct manner was not offensive like Rollo's or Cal's. And there was a lightness about her that wasn't *silly*.

'Yes. I'm hungry too.' Retra took a velvet dress from her drawer. It seemed modest enough. She glanced around for a changing cubicle but there was none.

Suki had already dropped her nightdress to the floor and had begun to wiggle her small, muscular body into a dark corset with a frilled trim that made it look like a skirt. Retra knew about corsets; her mother wore one. So did all the older Seal women. Her mother's corset was skin-coloured and serviceable; a brace. It had no frills or bows or lace.

'Hook me up, will you?' asked Suki.

Retra fumbled with the long laces, tying them inexpertly. Then she dressed, trying to hide her body from the others. 'Is it breakfast?'

Suki shrugged. 'Who knows? I guess it doesn't really matter when there's no daytime.' Her eyes sparkled. 'Wow! You look good in that. You need to let your hair down, though. It's a great colour. A real rich brown like your eyes.' She looked Retra up and down. 'How did they get the fit so right? It's magical ... the clothes and everything. I think I'm going to love this place.'

Retra straightened, catching her reflection in the mirror on the other wall. The velvet coated her body like honey. She felt more naked than the girl in the shawl. She reached into her drawer for another robe.

Suki grabbed her hand, her expression confused. 'Don't you want to look good?'

No, thought Retra. But the butterflies in her stomach said something else. *Yes*.

six

They entered one end of the cruciform and followed others heading to a curtained area. Suki linked arms with Retra as they passed through into a servery and a cluster of tables.

Her casual friendliness made Retra uneasy but she didn't draw away. Things would be different here. She must adapt.

Ripers watched them as the pair piled black linguine and a pink sauce onto brass platters and poured grape juice into thick-rimmed goblets.

'They give me the creeps,' whispered Suki.

Retra nodded, not trusting herself to speak. She couldn't rid herself of the notion that they could hear her, wherever they were. She shivered, remembering the Riper at the barge, and the voice in the dark. 'I met a girl on the barge who thought they were ... attractive.'

'Yeah, like bama droppings,' said Suki.

Retra reached the end of the meal line and glanced back along the row of silver hotplates. Who was serving the food? She hadn't noticed before but now that she was concentrating, she saw a small, furry, grey creature with a ladle in its prehensile paws.

She nudged Suki. 'What are they?'

Suki blinked a few times before she answered. 'Must be an uther. Charlonge told me they're hard to see. It's like they're invisible unless you concentrate on them.'

'She told you that?'

'Yeah. I had thousands of questions for her but she only answered a few.'

'For me too,' said Retra.

As they found a table and ate, Retra felt a pang of sympathy for Charlonge. How many new runaways had asked the same things? How many times had she given the same answers? And yet she had been patient with Retra, and gentle.

Suki sucked the last of the linguine off her fork, splashing her chin with the sauce. 'Nice chow,' she said, wiping her chin with the back of her hand.

Retra tried not to flinch. She wondered what Suki's home was like. Father would have punished her for such raw manners.

Charlonge entered and circled the tables with the air of a dormitory supervisor. She didn't stop to speak to Retra though her glance rested on her for a moment longer than necessary.

'They say she's been here for ages,' said Suki, watching Charlonge. 'That she's the oldest in Vank and should have gone ages ago.'

'Gone?'

Suki pulled a face at her. 'Didn't you know anything about this place before you came here?'

'Not really,' said Retra.

'When the Ripers decide you're too old to be here, they move you on somewhere else. They call it withdrawal.'

Retra felt a little surge of panic. Charlonge looked about the same age as Joel. What if Joel had already been withdrawn? 'Where do they move you to?'

'Nobody knows really but the Ripers say it's another island like this. I don't think it's an island, though. I bet they just take you out to the cusp of the Spiral and let you go.'

Retra picked up her plate and goblet and looked around for a place to rub them down.

'For agony's sakes,' Suki hissed. 'Leave them, Retra. The uthers will do it.'

Retra saw the smirks on the faces of those at nearby tables.

'Get it through your head,' said Suki. 'We don't have to do pig-cuss here. Ixion is just about fun and parties. Now let's go to confession so we can get out of here.'

Confession? Retra dropped the plate with a clatter, drawing the attention of one of the Ripers. She wanted to run from his penetrating stare but forced herself to copy Suki's jaunty stride as she got up and left the servery.

The cruciform was crowded now and Retra held her breath, automatically searching for Joel.

What if he is here? Now.

Suki grabbed her hand again and pointed towards the confessional queue. 'Over there.'

'Why do we need to confess if we can do what we like?'

Suki shrugged. 'Weird, huh? But that's what they told us we have to do. Maybe it's part of the cleansing. Like the re-birth.'

Retra noticed Cal at the head of the line, next to go in.

Suki saw her too. 'That one.' Suki pointed behind her hand at Cal. 'I hate her already.'

'H-has she been mean to you?'

Suki laughed. 'Nah. But she acts like she owns the guy on the guitar. And he is sooo hot. Why should she get dibs on him?' She pointed.

Retra looked over at the larger apse. The guitarist still sat atop the altar, backlit by glowing jewel lamps. Recognition made her pulse quicken. 'His name is Markes.'

'You know him?' Suki's eyes lit.

'I-I met him. That's all. On the barge.'

'You came by boat?'

Retra thought of the pain radiating along her leg when she left the Seal compound, and her desperate lunge to catch the barge. 'Why? How did you come?'

'You ever hear whirring in the sky?'

Retra nodded. 'Fly-eyes.'

Suki shook her head. 'Not always. Sometimes it's draculins. I trapped one in a cave outside my town, and strapped myself to its back.'

'What is a draculin?'

Suki rolled her eyes. 'You must know? Giant bat with wings bigger than ... two mountain bulls. They eat their own.'

'You mean echo-locaters?'

'Sure, if that's what you call them.'

'How did you know where the ... draculin you caught would go?'

'Don't you know anything? It's the lore. Draculins fly to Ixion in winter.'

Retra stared at the girl in amazement. 'But I've heard their bite will bleed you to death?'

Suki tossed her head airily. 'Uh-huh. But I'm here still.' She pushed Retra forward towards the confessional. 'Come on, you're next.'

Retra stepped cautiously into the small, dark cubicle. She was used to confession in Grave. The priest spoke through an electrified grille and arranged degrees of punishment depending on what she had the courage to confess. Usually he ordered denial: denial of food, or conversation, and sometimes sleep. When she'd confessed to listening to the *Angel Arias* he had prescribed six lashes of the snake whip.

Physical pain is the best form of purification, he'd said.

Her father had delivered the blows but the disappointment on his face had stung more than the lash. She'd cried all day.

As the confessional door snapped shut behind her a sweet, musty damp filled her lungs. Why would the Ripers wish to punish them already? Modesty is a sin, Charlonge had said.

Retra trembled, confused.

The grille slid back suddenly and she gasped.

The Riper from the barge sat there, his head disembodied by the small viewing window, his eyes as cold and seeking as before. 'What would be your pleasure, baby bat?'

'What do you ask me that? What should I confess?' she blurted.

'Your desires,' he hissed and tilted the window's ledge towards her. It unfolded into an elaborately worked drawer of many slots, each one containing a coloured shell, capsule, pod or bead. 'Pick your pleasure.'

'Are they medicines?'

His smile felt like a slimy, moist creature clambering over her body. 'Yes. If you like.'

Retra forced her fingers to the shelf. Fit in. Give them no reason to think you different ... She chose a pale rose pod, a less exotic colour than the others.

'Excellent,' he said. 'You must chew Rapture.'

Retra stood to leave but when she pushed the door it wouldn't open. She used her full strength on it before turning to the Riper.

'Chew it now!' His smile had gone, leaving only the chill stare.

Retra thought of resisting but claustrophobia sent a wave of panic clawing at her belly. He could keep her trapped here. He could ...

She placed the pod between her lips. It tasted as bitter as unripe lemon, and it crumbled in her mouth like cold, stale cake. She nibbled a little from the end.

'All of it,' he demanded. 'And hurry, baby bat, others are waiting. Or are you afraid of pleasure?'

'No. Of c-course not.' She forced the remainder of the pod into her mouth and chewed, swallowing it in rough lumps.

Suddenly, it seemed hard to breathe in the small cubicle. She longed for space and light, for the cool air of Grave with a tinge of rain. Her body felt overheated, the velvet clinging to her, prickling her skin.

'Don't stray from the lit paths, baby bat,' said the Riper.

Retra stood and pushed the door. It fell open easily this time and she stumbled out.

'Wait for me,' said Suki as she waltzed in.

But Retra had lost place and time. The cruciform of Vank began to shimmer around her, pulsing like an erratic and laboured heartbeat: closer then further. The candlelight streamed, bleeding upward to the arched wooden ribs and downward through the marbled floor.

With great care not to touch them, Retra moved between the rivers of lights towards the jewel-lit altar. The music drew her as if it were the cool spring rain she craved.

Markes already had an audience, a circle of admirers gathered at his feet. Cal sat there, closest to him.

Retra stepped into the centre of the circle of listeners, ignoring their calls for her to sit down.

Markes lifted his head from his guitar at the sight of her. *What?* He mouthed the question.

In reply, she arched her back and lifted her hands to her hips.

His sharp intake of breath told her that he saw what she was about to do. His eyes fixed on her as she yielded to a building desire. She wanted to touch Markes, feel his hair, touch her fingers to his lips. Her body ached to be close to him.

She took a step forward. Another one. Picking her way through the circle until she stood before him and his guitar. She couldn't see anyone else now. The rest of the world had become a dark, narrow place with Markes the point of light. 'You,' she said. 'Me.'

But the words seemed to make the darkness swirl and toss her around. Markes shrank in her vision, becoming smaller, less wondrous, less ...

Someone shook her: angry and sharp, as if to rattle her to pieces.

'Stop it!' shouted Cal. 'Go away. Leave him alone.' She forced Retra back from the altar like an overzealous guard.

Markes climbed down, his guitar hanging at his side and his brow wrinkled with concern. 'Retra, are you sick?'

She couldn't answer him. Nor could she feel her feet or her knees or the flesh in between. Strange shapes formed, collecting either side of Markes: wings and claws and long, slavering tongues. She put her hands up to bat them away.

'What is it?' cried Markes. 'What can you see?'

'More like what did you take,' said another voice. Suki's almond eyes swam into her view.

'Suki, do you see them – the claws?' Retra whispered.

Suki's fingers gripped her arm, nails biting her skin. 'Don't see nothin' but him.' She fluttered her eyes. 'And I don't mind looking at that.'

Markes frowned. 'What did you say about claws? What –'

But then Cal and the crowd closed in on them, collecting Markes, urging him back to his guitar and the altar, and expunging Retra and Suki in their wake.

As Markes climbed back to his seat the claws and wings vanished and Retra sagged back against Suki with relief. The world had come back, the smell of incense and the murmur of voices.

'Markes,' voices carolled. 'Play for us. Play ...'

A girl in black silk shorts and a metallic tank top jumped up alongside him. 'I'll dance for you.'

Cal tugged the girl down. 'No you won't.'

The girl slapped at Cal but Cal ducked and kicked her ankle. Arms grabbed at them and bodies moved in between until Retra could barely see Cal or the girl at all.

Suki forced a beaker of water into Retra's hand. 'Here.'

She drank it, coughing a little. The water sank heavily onto her stomach and she pressed her hand to her mouth.

'You gonna be sick?'

Retra nodded.

Suki pointed to a small, dark apse furnished with a large urn to one side of the side of the altar. 'In there.'

Retra ran a few steps and sank her face into the urn, heaving the water up. Her sight cleared properly and she realised her velvet dress had ridden up high on her hips and that her hair had come loose. She wrenched her dress down over her thighs, humiliated, and retied her hair.

'Better?' asked Suki. She stood behind her, unfazed by the vomit.

'I think so. I'm sorry.'

Suki shrugged. 'People get sick. I've nursed plenty of 'em. What did you take?'

'A Rapture p-pod.'

'How much of it?'

'He-he told me to eat it all.'

'Modai gave you a whole rapture pod? No wonder you were about to do the la la.'

'Is that the Riper's name?'

'Yeah, 'parently. Someone in the line told me about him while you were in there. Asmodai is the demon of lust and wrath and this guy is supposed to be his half-mortal son. Fits him, don't you think?' She glanced around. 'The uthers will clean this up. Come on, let's get out of here.'

Retra got to her feet and followed Suki out of the cruciform, leaving Markes and his audience behind them.

Outside, different noises filled the damp air; not the normal night owl sounds Retra heard in Grave. These were more guttural, deeper.

The climb to the platform seemed endless, the stairs stretching further and further before them. She grasped the handrail with both hands, using the solidity of the iron to guide her.

'How do you feel now?' Suki asked when they reached the top. She held Retra's arm firmly, keeping her away from the edge.

'Dizzy.'

'You're s'posed to have the pod in pieces over a week – or at least a few days.'

'How do you know that?'

'Modai told me. Besides, it's common sense. Just like taking our rock algae medicines at home. They mess with your head. Too much and you'll eat rat gizzards thinking it's sweet goo-berry pie.'

Retra stared over at the dark edge of the platform. It beckoned to her but this time she resisted. 'I think I'll sit down.' She tottered to a bench seat, welcoming the hard wood underneath her. 'I feel strange still. Not myself.'

'Well, while you are someone else,' said Suki, dancing a few steps along the platform, 'let's party.'

seven

Suki talked about her home as the cable kar looped back onto the main lines and up the face of the crater. She chatted, feet up on the seat, admiring the twists of leather and lace on her new boots.

'My town is called Stra'ha. It's the highest town on the Stra'haman trail before the high path to the ranges. It's so boring there, except for the caves. Draculins by the million.' Her expression became wicked, one eyebrow cocked. 'I signed a pact once in draculin blood with a boy from the low towns. He came to visit with his father to sell arms to the women.'

'Women don't use weapons in Grave. We're not permitted to do ... group things.' Retra heard her own voice speaking sensibly yet the words might have come from another's mouth. Her body and mind went through the actions of being her, but her deep mind, her imagination wandered elsewhere. In her hindbrain colours bled as she looked out into the night, and sounds thickened into lumps that she wanted to chew and crunch.

'Grave. Yeah, I heard about that place from a boy at the re-birth. He was a kinda cute red-head. Sounds kinda weird there. He said you aren't allowed to talk to others in groups in case you get outta control. You can't dance or play music. Some places there are even worse than that apparently – they barely talk at all.'

Retra nodded, not wanting to admit she was from one of them.

'Anyway, there are only women in Stra'ha. It's a woman's town. The men don't do so well with the altitude. It makes their spermies go sterile. The women have to go to the low towns to breed but they always come back to Stra'ha. They need to protect the men from the raiders who come across the ranges in summer or our people would die out.'

'The women protect the men?'

Suki looked at her. 'Of course! Is it different for you?'

'My father makes all the decisions in our house.'

'In Stra'ha we only need the men for their spermies, otherwise ... pffft.'

Retra's face burned at the thought. 'Why did you come here then?'

'Like I said ... it was boring. And Liam ... the boy I blooded with ... he was coming here. We said we'd meet.'

'Did he come? Have you seen him?'

'He'll be here. You can't lie to a person when you've crossed with echo blood.' But Suki looked uncertain for a moment.

They sat in silence for a while and Retra's mind was caught up marvelling at a band of vivid golden spirals dancing across the walls of the kar. She wanted to ask Suki if she saw them too, but was afraid she would sound crazy.

Then the kar arrived at a station, groaning as it slowed.

A group wearing white bandanas crowded through the open doors and Suki put her feet down to make room. They were laughing and singing and Retra wanted to rake her fingers through their words and lick them. She felt sure they would be juicy, tender in her mouth.

A girl tumbled onto the seat in front of them. Hair redder than Rollo's spilled out of her bandana, and she wore purple eye shadow up to the top of her eyebrows. Others went to sit next to her, then hesitated and moved on.

As the tram doors began to close, a boy with spiky hair half-hidden underneath a white bandana sprang onto the bottom step. He slid his muscular arm between the doors, and the sensors froze them, halting the kar.

He took his time climbing the remaining steps, looking around, checking out who was on board.

A few of the other boys called to him and he saluted them. His movements were slow and deliberate, demanding attention; his hair shone as slick as the seaweed that washed up on Grave's rocky beaches.

Retra had kept some seaweed from her last trip to the beach, years ago, back when Joel wasn't much taller than her and her mother still smiled.

The boy dropped heavily into the seat in front of them, next to the red-headed girl.

'Some entrance. He must practise it,' said Suki too loudly.

The boy swivelled round and stared at them. A quiet descended on the kar.

'What's ya name?' he asked.

'Suki.'

'You gotta mouth, Suki. You wanna watch yourself.'

Suki bristled. 'You should do the same.'

Retra was suddenly stuck by a premonition. She had to intervene. Prevent the rift. 'Suki's from Stra'ha,' she said, suddenly. 'She's used to … telling males what to do.'

The boy's gaze shifted to her. His eyes showed intelligence and a lot of pride. 'Who're you?'

'Retra.' She held out her hand. 'I'm from Seal South. But you can't catch it.'

'It?'

'Being a Seal.'

He stared at her a moment longer and then he laughed. He didn't take her hand but he turned back and slouched down in his seat.

Everyone around them fell to talking again and Suki's shoulders relaxed.

Retra's premonition slipped away.

The red-headed girl with the heavy eye make-up climbed up on her knees and leaned over the back of her seat. She pointed sideways at the guy. 'He's Kero. He runs the White Wings,' she said. 'I'm Krista-belle. I'm with him.' She sounded proud about that.

'What're White Wings?' asked Suki.

'Our gang. There are others too. White Wings, Ghosts and Freeks. We're named after bats, but only the ones that suck blood.' Her eyes glittered. 'You'll learn about 'em soon enough. Whites are the best though. We look after our own. Ghosts take anyone in, no trial, and no questions. And the Freeks are rad.'

Retra heard without really listening. The girl's words were taking shapes, flying from her mouth like butterflies. She wanted to reach out and catch them in her hand.

'Main thing you newbies have to remember is to stay on the main strip. Don't go walking the Lesser Paths.'

'People disappear on the paths,' added a guy from across the aisle. His head was shaved under his bandana. He sat on a girl's knee and she groaned and giggled with the weight of him. 'Even the League can't save them.'

'The League's fearsome,' his girl said.

'No more fearsome than us.'

The girl poked out her tongue. 'Clash's way more fearsome than you.'

The guy ground his buttocks on the girl's knee, making her groan louder.

Retra forced her lips to make the word shapes. 'Who's Clash?'

'You are brand newbies, aren't you?'

Before Suki or Retra could reply, Krista-belle clicked her long painted fingernails against the metal-work of the seat, calling attention back her way. She gave a smile that made Retra think of something warm and soft. 'Ruzalia the pirate's snatching Peaks – over-agers – and a new gang's helping her do it. They're calling themselves the Cursed League, run by Dark Eve and Clash. She's huge, like a freaking bear, and he's ... hot.'

'Settle down.' Kero slapped her lazily on the rump.

Krista-belle giggled. 'When the Ripers catch up with them, they'll be gone. Withdrawn early. Pfft!'

'Clash and his gang can't be too smart then. Sounds like a stupid, dangerous thing to do,' said Suki.

'The League say they're thinking ahead. I mean, we all get to be Peaks eventually and the League thinks that withdrawal means abandoned, thrown off the island into some kind of wasteland. If they're right, I don't want to be wasted. I'd rather be with Ruzalia.'

'What if they're wrong? And why did you come here if you're so scared of aging?' Retra could tell Suki was angry still. Little waves of it rolled off her.

'Didn't seem to matter when I was a newbie. Getting older seemed so far away. I've been here a while now, though. You start thinking about it. 'Specially when you see others disappear.'

'Maybe being withdrawn means you get sent to paradise,' said Suki.

'We're already in paradise,' said the shaved-head guy. He poked his tongue out and waggled it around. It was stained black. He stuck it into the mouth of the girl he sat on. She gagged and dumped him on the floor of the aisle. Then she sat on him and stuck her tongue down his throat.

Everyone laughed at them.

Krista-belle hung further over their seat. 'Hope you've got that right, Suki. But just in case you haven't, I'm backing Ruzalia and the League ...' She rolled her eyes and dropped back down next to Kero.

He moved closer and let his head fall down onto her shoulder.

In a few more stops someone called out, 'It's the Drop.'

The White Wings piled out, leaving the kar almost empty.

Retra stood up and the world swayed. Golden spirals swirled across everyone, spinning on their skin and their faces, disappearing into their mouths. She thought she might be sick again. 'Let's get off here too,' she said thickly. She needed to walk and breathe.

Suki shrugged and followed her off the kar.

Retra walked along a wooden bridge that led from the platform straight into the top storey of a square stone building.

Suki reached for her hand. Retra had never held a girl's hand before today. Seals didn't touch each other very much. Mother had kissed her goodnight when she was young. That's all she could remember. Yet, somehow, Suki's touch made her feel better.

Now that she was moving, the spirals had disappeared and sounds had become merely sounds again, not something she wanted to eat.

Ripers stood waiting and watching on either side of the entrance to the club. One of them wore her hair in long black and white streaks. Her face was heavily scarred.

'There's Brand,' whispered Suki. 'She was on stage with Lenoir and Test at the re-birth. She's creepy. All those marks on her skin.'

Brand. Retra remembered her. The one who'd torn away her veil and tunic after Lenoir had spoken to them.

As they walked past the scarred Riper, Retra's fingers tightened on Suki's. She couldn't help it. It was that, or run back to the kar.

The Stra'ha girl squeezed back. 'It's okay,' she whispered. 'They're here to keep us safe.'

Once they were inside, though, Suki let go of her hand and began to jig. 'Aaah ... listen ... I die over this song.' She ran off ahead.

Retra followed more slowly, taking in the top floor scaffolding and the ceiling decorated with light-reflecting streamers, and glitter globes that floated above her head. The balls shot off little beams, casting dotted patterns on the faces and limbs of the dancers below. An open-cage lift crawled up and down the side of the scaffolding, depositing newcomers on the dance floor on the bottom level and then returning to the top. On the other end of the floor was a narrow set of spiral stairs, but no one seemed to be bothering to use them, preferring to hang over the sides of the crowded cage.

Suki glanced back at her once. 'Don't leave without me,' she shouted, before she ran onto the lift.

Retra watched her go, unsure of what to do next. The lighting was dimmer than Vank. Perhaps she could stay unnoticed and wait for Suki to tire of the place. But something about the music was impossible to ignore. The drumbeat crept into her chest and along her limbs. Like Markes's guitar, it made her body want to move.

She caught the next lift down, drawn to the source of it. Standing on the edge of the dance floor, she sensed the current feeding backward and forward among the dancers, skittering along their laughter and their casual embraces, linking them together.

Some boy grabbed her arm. 'Come on,' he urged.

She let him lead her out to the dance floor. The music seemed deeper, thicker out there. When she tried to copy the boy her movements were stiff, and clumsy, as if she'd been cramped in a small compartment for some time and now, suddenly, had been given space to move.

The boy spun and jumped in front of her, encouraging her.

She slowly followed his lead, letting her limbs loosen.

Then the beat changed, pulsing faster and faster. The crowd surged in close and in one accord they began to jump, forcing her to do the same or be crushed. She bathed in the energy pouring forth from the moving bodies. Her heart beat wildly and heat radiated from the top of her head like a burning halo. Her hair came loose; bodies banged against her, and bore her up and down as if suddenly they were one dancer, one sound, one heartbeat.

She tore the band from her hair.

A heart that beat forever; music that went on forever. So long that she lost her place in time, so long that even her altered metabolism began to tire, so long …

And then, finally, it stopped. The music ended – torn away from her.

The crowd slowed and broke apart, disorientated, lost without their purpose. Retra clung to the feeling, wanting it back. She had never felt so bright before, so shiny and large. But the boy she'd been dancing with had disappeared and the palm of her hand felt hot. She glanced at the faux badge. Had she been dancing for so long that she needed to rest already?

Disconsolate and lost, she drifted among the crowd who'd gravitated to the drink stations. She looked at faces hoping to see Joel. But her head felt muzzy and the dimness made it hard to see faces properly.

She took the cage lift back to the top level and wandered out through the entrance. Though the Ripers still leaned near the door, Brand was no longer among them and their scrutiny made her nervous.

Should she return to Vank and rest? Or wait for Suki? The Stra'ha girl seemed so much nicer than Cal, but they'd still only just met. Was it possible to make friends so quickly? In Grave, the Seal girls only talked to each other when walking to and from Disciplines.

One of them – Toola – would wait for her by the skeleton tree after prayers, and they would sit together and share goat cheese and sweetbreads. Toola always asked her about Joel; what he was like, what he talked about. Her eyes would shine when Retra answered.

Then Joel left, and the warden was assigned to Retra's family. Toola shunned her. After that she walked and ate alone.

Retra's thoughts shifted to Joel. If *he'd* asked her to wait somewhere then she would. Using that as her guide, Retra turned back into the club to wait for Suki, but instead of catching the lift, she walked across to the less-crowded spiral stairs.

As she descended, the music bombarded her mind again, but the effects of the Rapture pod seemed to have waned, and she felt less inclined to dance. The badge on her palm still throbbed hotly, reminding her that she needed to rest.

She peered through the gloom behind the stairs. The crowds were thinner under this end of the dais, spread among tables and stools. Screens ran across the back wall, jutting out in L shapes. She walked over and looked behind one.

A couple was lying on a couch. Retra saw their legs entwined and their hands moving inside each other's clothing.

She backed out, shocked.

'Whatcha doin', Retra-Seal?' said a slurry voice, in her ear.

Retra jumped. It was Krista-belle from the kar; one of the White Wings. The girl swayed, as if she was having trouble keeping her balance, and her breath smelt strange, like burnt oranges.

'Have you seen the girl I was with? Suki?' Retra asked her.

The girl shook her head and pointed. 'Jus' gonna have a little lie down in there. Not feeling so good.'

'Where's your ... where's Kero?'

'Can't find him.' She shrugged unhappily and staggered off behind one of the screens.

Retra thought about following her to see if she was all right, then changed her mind. She'd just met Krista-belle; she didn't need to watch over her. Instead, she walked a circuit of the dance floor looking for Suki, but it was more crowded than before. She ended up back in the same spot in front of the screens.

Her palm was stinging now. She had to leave. Perhaps she could ask Krista-belle to tell Suki that she'd gone back to Vank.

She went over to the screen and knocked.

When there was no answer, she looked behind it. She couldn't see Krista-belle but a Riper lay on a couch with her back to Retra, her coat and boots a stark outline against the pale covering.

As Retra began to retreat, a movement caught her attention. The glimpse of a frantic hand, fist closed and pumping, beating at the Riper's back.

Krista-belle's hand.

Retra knew what that movement meant. She'd used it on the warden, in her dreams, beating at his head as he held her down to inspect her thigh.

She took a few steps closer. Music drowned voices. Shadows cloaked detail. But she saw the side of the Riper's scarred face clearly enough.

Brand.

She wanted to run away from what was happening but she couldn't. She *knew* that frenzied movement. The cold fear in her belly warmed, and then slowly began to boil. She tried to contain the angry welling with Seal discipline; tried to quiet her thoughts.

Calm is my reward.

Calm is my reward.

She'd never shown her anger when her father had whipped her. Or when he'd denied her food as penance. Even when the warden pawed at her thigh, and the softer parts around it, she'd never let her control slip ...

Calm is my reward.

Calm is my –

But this time her mantra failed her. The sight of Brand smothering Krista-belle set loose a fury in her that deepened and widened with each breath. She hadn't been able to stop the warden but she could –

The Riper shifted, crouching over the girl's exposed breast. Krista-belle's red hair spilled out as she strained away, face contorted with terror.

Retra ran out into the club, looking for something – anything. She snatched up a stool and returned with it lifted high above her head.

'Stop!' she cried.

But the Riper didn't hear her, or chose not to.

'Please ... stop!'

Nothing. Just Kristabelle's panic and revulsion, and the Riper's sickening intent.

Anger raged through Retra. Clutching the stool tightly, she brought it down as hard as she could onto Brand's back.

The Riper arched back in pained surprise. She rolled off the couch, unnaturally quick and agile, her mouth open, teeth bared.

Retra froze in the grip of her bestial stare.

Freed of Brand's hold, Krista-belle gave a high-pitched scream that rang above the beat of the music. As Brand stalked towards Retra, Krista-belle scrambled off the couch and ran past them both, out into the club.

Retra turned to follow her but Brand seized her wrist, twisting it.

'It seems that you will have to do instead, baby bat,' said the Riper.

The Riper pulled Retra towards the couch with an unnatural strength. Her cruel fingers wrenched Retra's chin up, exposing her throat. Brand's face lowered towards hers. 'I remember you at re-birth, little one. You ran away from me.' The Riper made a noise of satisfaction.

Retra writhed to escape the nearness of the Riper's scarred face; the thick, damaged ridges of skin along her cheek and forehead that bespoke something ugly and dire.

'But not this time,' Brand whispered.

Pale teeth scraped along Retra's neck and a camphor scent overwhelmed her. Her lungs filled with it, struggling to find air above the sharp, pervasive odour. Fingers gripped her thighs, up under her dress, forcing her legs apart, and she felt the sharp pain of something puncturing her skin under her jaw line.

Then, without warning, the Riper's weight was gone.

Retra lifted her head and looked up. The club had gone silent; music dead, lights brighter.

'Brand?' Lenoir's unmistakable voice sounded in Retra's ear, in her head. 'What goes on here?'

Brand rolled onto her feet in one movement.

The booth was filled with people: Lenoir, Brand, Test and more Ripers. One of them held Kero around the neck as he made futile efforts to get free. Krista-belle and the White Wings pressed in around and behind them.

'*What* are you doing with the girl, Brand?' Lenoir again.

Brand hunched her leather-clad shoulders and curled her lips in a sneer. 'Nothing.'

'You know that it's forbidden to touch the younglings.' Lenoir's voice was quiet but intense as it entered Retra's mind. She couldn't drag her eyes from him. This close he was breathtaking; tall and lean, with sleek hair falling below his shoulders. His skin was whiter than Cal's hair, and his face was made beautiful by the perfect symmetry of his features.

'You think you need to preach our rules to me, Lenoir?'

'I think you forgot yourself. That wouldn't happen again, *would it?*'

Lenoir's last two words hung heavily between them.

'The first girl was a mistake. I was needy,' Brand allowed. 'But this one ...' She pointed to Retra. 'This one attempted to harm me. What would you have me do?'

'Harm?' Lenoir looked at Retra, the fallen stool, and Brand. 'How truly terrifying for you.'

The Ripers around Lenoir didn't hide their smirks.

Brand bared her teeth again and swept out of the booth, knocking aside the rest of the White Wings who crowded around the edge of the screen, trying to see in. Their cries of protest went unheeded by Lenoir.

He glided closer to Retra, his gaze scalding her. 'You show courage, little bat, to protect a friend, and foolishness. Never attempt such a thing again. We have ways to manage such an occurrence.'

Part of Retra wanted to disappear beneath his stare, but her anger was still alive and fanning a stubbornness that would not let her submit. 'Such an occurrence? But I thought you were our Guardians. Our safekeepers.'

'We are. That's why I am here and why you are still alive.' He turned to Kero. 'This is finished. Take your gang and leave.'

The Riper holding Kero let go and, as quickly as they'd appeared, Lenoir and his Guardians left, leaving Retra alone with the White Wings.

Krista-belle launched herself at Retra straightaway, clutching her tight. 'Thank you,' she sobbed.

Retra stood awkwardly in the girl's grip until Kero pulled his girlfriend back under his arm. He looked upset, his expression caught between anger and distress.

'Seal Retra?'

Retra nodded. The palm of her hand was so hot now that it burned, and weariness fell across her like a thick blanket.

'Let me through!' Another voice penetrated through the quiet group.

Suki pushed her way in to stand next to Retra. Her makeup had smeared, and one stocking had laddered. 'What's up? What's going on?' She gave Kero a furious glance. 'What've you done to her?'

'Nothin',' croaked out Kero.

He stepped closer to Retra so that he, Krista-belle, Suki and she were in a tight circle. 'Seal or not, we owe you for this.'

Retra tried to think of something to say, but her palm felt as if it had caught fire and the room had started to spin. Her only coherent thought fixed on Suki's concern. No one had shown her that since Joel. Even Mother ... Mother had been too scared.

'What's wrong with her?' someone asked.

Suki grabbed her hand and held it, palm up, next to her own. 'Ret, you've gotta rest now. Real quick.'

'Find me later and we'll talk,' said Kero.

But Suki shook her head. 'Forget later, tough guy. You gotta help me get her back to Vank. *Now*.'

eight

'She's fortunate. The Guardians allow some room for mistakes among the newcomers. If she does this again, though, her time here will be shortened,' she drew a breath, 'or snuffed out completely. *Petite nuit must* be observed.'

Retra recognised Charlonge's sombre voice without having to open her eyes.

'I'll tell her.' And Suki.

'Krista-belle, you should know better than to let one of your own miss *petite nuit*,' scolded Charlonge.

'It was Brand's fault,' argued Krista-belle. 'We were at the Drop. Kero was talking to Juice from the Freeks and I felt sick. I went to lie down on one of the couches. You know, behind the wall screens, where couples go to catch some down time. Brand found me. She ... she ... climbed on me and ...' Krista-belle faltered.

'Brand? But the Ripers are forbidden to have any physical contact with us. It's lore. They're our Guardians.' Charlonge sounded puzzled.

'She's been watching me for a while. I thought it was because I'm getting older. You never really know when it will be your time.'

'You should go to the Youth Circle and tell them what happened. You must speak up.'

Krista-belle made a rude noise. 'What's the point? What would they do? Tell Lenoir? He already knows. He stopped Brand from hurting Retra after she threw the stool.'

'She threw a stool?'

'Right at Brand's back. Smashed it into her.'

Retra sensed Charlonge's astonishment in the silence that followed.

'Lenoir said he would protect us. But I'm not so sure, Char.' Krista-belle's voice quavered when she eventually spoke. 'Something's happening with the Ripers. I mean ... among them. I can feel it. Kero says the Freeks have noticed it. He's going to talk to the Ghosts too. We think something's going to happen soon. Not something good either.'

'You're imagining things.' Charlonge's tone was sharper. 'And such talk can be seen as troublemaking. Speak to the Circle about the incident with Brand, let them deal with it. Otherwise keep your mouth shut. And you too, Suki. You're too new here to be involved in this kind of thing. You'll be tainted by it. Now, I have to go and supervise mealtime. Bring her down when she is rested.'

Retra waited until the door closed before she rolled over. Her eyes met Suki's straightaway. The Stra'ha girl was sitting on a chair close to her. She was wearing a lace shirt and short pants, and chewing her fingernails. Krista-belle was at the foot of the bed, in a simple red velvet dress that set off her hair. They were in a room with a single bed, furnished with only a small table weighed by an untidy pile of old books.

'We're in Charlonge's room,' said Suki. 'She said it was best not to draw attention to you.'

'You feeling better, Retra?' asked Krista-belle.

Like Suki she'd changed clothes since the club, but her eye shadow was still heavily purple and her lashes thick with paint.

Retra nodded, and levered upward to lean against the heavy bed head. The nubs of iron studs stuck into her back, and she rearranged the pillows to cushion them. Then she looked at her palm. The colour had faded again, leaving only the tattooed outline of the badge.

'I'm well,' she reassured them, feeling the heat rising in her cheeks at the unaccustomed attention. 'Th-thank you for bringing me back here.'

'Kero and the boys carried you,' said Krista-belle proudly.

'You zoned out in the club,' added Suki. She sounded a little sour. 'I told them they had to help, seeing as what you did for them.'

But Suki's flat expression didn't seem to have an effect on Krista-belle. The red-head jumped up from her seat and clasped Retra's hand. 'Kero's down in the refectory. He wants to talk to you about joining the Wings. You can be one of us.'

Retra stared at her and then at Suki.

Suki shrugged. 'They said I could too. Because of you.'

Krista-belle's hand felt warm and sticky against Retra's skin. 'I-I don't know. What do you do?' Retra asked.

'Oh,' she said vaguely, 'the usual. We go out in groups. Make sure no one gets forgotten and strays onto the Lesser Paths. Mostly, it's just fun. Hanging out. We look out for each other. That's the best thing. Though sometimes the boys fight against the other gangs.'

'What do they fight about?'

She picked at her black-painted fingernails. 'Stuff. Who's tougher, I guess.'

Retra didn't like the sound of it but Suki's eyes lit up. 'Fighting?'

Krista-belle tugged Retra's hand. 'Come and talk to Kero, please.'

'Yeah,' said Suki. 'Geddup! I'm getting bored here.'

The pair followed Retra down to the *neglegere*, chatting about music, and Brand, and boys, while she washed and put on the fresh clothes from her locker; black net stockings this time, with a soft, clinging tunic and boots. Retra's boots on Grave were the walking kind, not high-heeled and running up above her knee. She tried to fold the top back and Suki slapped her hand away.

'Leave them alone,' she said. 'They're supposed to be like that.'

'They feel strange,' she said.

'Sexy,' giggled Krista-belle. 'You'd better watch out.'

Retra wondered if Markes would like them then chided herself for such a shallow thought. Joel was the most important thing in her life. She had to find him and then … and then what? Persuade him to leave Ixion. They would go somewhere else, together. Not Grave, but one of the places that Charlonge had spoken about. 'I'm ready,' she said.

The refectory was crowded with newbies and White Wings. A glance at Charlonge standing over by the servery with her hands clasped tight told Retra that the Vank supervisor was tense. She was staring at Kero, who sat with his feet up on a table, talking to a couple of Wings – boys, older than Retra.

Krista-belle took Retra's hand and led her through the table-maze to her boyfriend. Suki trailed behind them and Retra sensed her reluctance. From what Suki had said, she was used to fighting, and men kept to their place in her province. Here, things were different.

'Kero, look!' said Krista-belle. She pulled Retra forward. 'She's okay.'

Kero nodded at one of the empty chairs. 'Siddown, girls.'

Retra perched on the edge of a chair, uncomfortable with the attention the whole refectory was giving them, including Charlonge.

There was a moment of awkward silence before Kero mumbled, 'Glad you're okay.'

'Thank you,' she answered.

'So … like I said before in the club … what you did for Krissie was … well … ballsy. Normally we don't take Seals in the Wings but you can join us if you want.' He flicked a glance to Suki, who was standing behind Retra. 'Her too.'

'Don't do me any favours,' said Suki, sulkily.

Kero shrugged. 'Suit yourself.'

Retra practised her answer in her head a couple of times before she spoke. She wanted her voice steady and Kero made her nervous. She knew her expression would be calm, at least. Seals knew how to do that.

'Your offer is kind but I don't want to join *anyone*. There is something, though ...' She hesitated. 'Can we talk about it ... alone?'

Kero slid his feet down and sprawled forwards, elbows on the table. 'Go mingle, lads,' he told the other guys.

His gangers got up and left, making rude signs to him behind their hands, so the girls couldn't see, as they walked away. Kero laughed.

Krista-belle sat down next to him, but Suki stayed where she was, behind Retra's shoulder, hands on hips.

'Spit it out,' said Kero.

'I'm looking for someone called Joel. He's tall and thin with brown hair. He came here nearly a year ago.'

Krista-belle clapped her hands. 'You're in love! Like me and Kero!'

'Krissie,' growled Kero in warning.

Krista-belle licked her lips and made a kissing noise.

Kero gave her a fierce frown but Krista-belle just kept on grinning.

Retra could feel Suki trembling behind her. She glanced over her shoulder. The girl was trying not to laugh.

'He's not my b-boyfriend,' said Retra. 'But I want to ... I must find him.'

Kero chewed his lip for a moment. 'There're more than a thousand of us on Ixion. Chance is he's changed his name. Most do. Might not look the same anymore, either. He might have even been withdrawn. Happens all the time.'

'No!' Retra reared up from her chair.

'Whoa. Settle,' said Kero, tilting back in his seat. 'Can you tell me anything else about him?'

Retra took a breath and thought for a moment. 'He speaks his mind. He's not afraid. Not like most Seals.' Not like me. Unbidden tears stung the back of her eyes. *I must not cry*. Not in front of these people.

If Kero saw her emotion, he didn't react.

Krista-belle clasped her hand again. 'You're plenty strong-willed,' she said. 'You smacked out a Riper to help me. Most of the guys on Ixion wouldn't have the guts to do that.'

Kero glowered at her this time, but Krista-belle didn't seem to be the kind of person to worry too much about quelling looks. Her bright eyes were riveted upon Retra with unmistakable admiration and gratitude.

Retra's discomfort deepened. She wanted to be free of this conversation and the sparring between Kero and Krista-belle. 'Can you help me find Joel?'

Kero shrugged; his favourite gesture.

Retra counted several breaths then got up to leave.

'Wait,' he said. 'Look, no promises but ... can you keep something to yourselves?'

Retra waited.

'There's a meeting of the gangs right after the next Early-Eve. It's real important that the Ripers don't find out about it.'

'When's Early-Eve? I've heard of it but no one has explained.'

Kero made an impatient noise and tugged on this hair. He looked at Krista-belle for help.

'Because we don't have night and day, we call things differently here. Twice in every twenty-six hours, the darkness lifts a little. Not sunlight, of course, but something more ... dusky. The lightest of the two is called Early-Eve, the other one is called Night-Eve,' Krista-belle explained.

'Oh. And the meeting?'

Kero leaned forward. 'The meeting's about *them*. Krissie's not the first one Brand's touched. We've gotta work out what to do about it,' he said, in a lowered voice. 'Thanks to you, at least Lenoir knows about Brand now. Not that we think he'll do anything about it.'

Hearing Lenoir's name gave Retra a shiver. 'What about the Youth Circle? Lenoir said that you should tell them. So did Charlonge.'

'Wasters,' said Kero.

'Too busy taking black beads and sucking up to Varonessa and Lenoir,' concurred Krista-belle.

'Why should I come to the meeting? Do you think Joel will be there?'

'You said he was outspoken. If he is, then he's probably joined one of the gangs, and they'll all be at the meeting. If you come along, you might recognise him.'

Retra nodded slowly. Kero's logic made sense to her. 'After next Early-Eve?'

'Yeah,' said Kero. 'In the Grotto.' He beckoned her to lean down closer.

Retra bent stiffly, until her ear was near his mouth.

'Password to get past the gate is "the-age-of-rage",' he said.

She nodded and straightened. 'Thank you.'

'Kero will help you find him. Kero knows everyone,' said Krista-belle. She leaned across and pulled her boyfriend into her arms, wiggling her tongue out near his lips.

He opened his mouth and latched onto it, making loud sucking noises.

'Gross,' announced Suki.

Retra looked at her.

Suki inclined her head. 'Let's get some food.'

'You gonna go to this meeting?' asked Suki through a mouthful of streaky bacon and red chilli beans.

The pair had taken seats at the table furthest from the refectory curtain. While they'd piled food on their plates at the servery, the White Wings had drifted out, following Kero and Krista-belle, leaving only a handful of newbies at the tables. Though they were still getting curious glances from them, at least Charlonge had stopped hovering.

Retra nodded. She'd chosen a bowl of sweetened meal and some wisp bread. The bread melted on her tongue like buttery air. She glanced over at the servery looking for the uther. By concentrating hard, she could see it scraping egg-mash from one silvery dish to another. Did they do the cooking, she wondered? She imagined the dough in their thin, grey, prehensile fingers and felt a little squeamish.

'So who's Joel?' Suki was still asking questions.

Retra hesitated.

'Come on, I told you about Liam and our blood pact,' said Suki.

Retra glanced around. There was no one close enough to hear their conversation. It went against all her Seal instincts to tell Suki more about Joel, but Krista-belle and

Kero knew of him now. Suki had been nothing but kind to her and Retra liked the way she spoke her mind. Envied it, in fact.

'He's my brother,' she whispered.

'Oh?' Suki chewed for a bit. 'Well, I guess that's happened before. Sisters following brothers here, and the other way around. My sister is a *shicka*. I wouldn't follow her to the end of the road.'

Retra raised her eyebrows.

'A stay-at-home type. Likes to cook and grow high-country lavender,' Suki finished.

Retra wanted to explain to Suki that she hadn't followed Joel here to be part of Ixion, but to convince him to go somewhere else. But even Suki's forthrightness and honesty couldn't convince her to share that. 'Other sisters following their brothers?. I suppose so.'

Suki slapped her head in mock exasperation. 'You gotta start talking less stiff. You sound so old. Like my Granna. It's "I guess so", not "I sup-pose so".'

Retra smiled. 'I suppose it is.'

They both laughed.

For Suki the sound came out easy and naturally. For Retra it was like opening the door of a cage that had been closed for too long; an uncertain, rusty sound.

Suki whacked her on the back as if she was choking.

And then they laughed more.

Until Charlonge appeared at their table.

The tension still played through the supervisor's body. Retra could see it in her stiff shoulders and neck. 'What were the White Wings saying to you?'

Retra stared at her bowl but Suki spoke up.

'They just wanted to thank Retra for helping Kristabelle out. And they asked us to join the Wings.'

Retra wished Suki would be quiet and stop telling Charlonge everything. But it wasn't in the Stra'ha girl's nature to be silent.

Charlonge drew a chair back and sat down with them. She folded her hands inside the long sleeves of her dress. 'That wouldn't be wise.'

Her counsel made Retra curious even though she had no plans to join the Wings. 'Why not? It seems like a place to belong. As good as another,' she said softly. It was the truth. There was something alluring in the way they banded together.

'Ixion is a place of freedom and expression. The White Wings and the others impose their own rules. Why would you want that? Especially coming from a province like Grave. Besides, the Ripers only tolerate the gangs, but they don't approve of them. You will attract more attention to yourself by joining one. It seems you have done enough to be monitored already.'

Retra thought of the warden at home in Grave. 'What happens when you're monitored?'

'The Ripers watch you. Everywhere you go. *Everywhere.*'

As if hearing Charlonge, Forlorn entered the refectory, his sweeping gaze pausing to linger on them.

Charlonge got to her feet again. 'Brand won't forget what you did,' she whispered. 'Be careful.' She moved to another table and sat down with the girls Retra had seen in the dressing room earlier.

'She's right about one thing,' said Suki. 'Brand is scary – all those scars and things. It might be safer being part of the Wings.'

Retra didn't answer.

'Oh, well,' said Suki, stuffing the last of the bacon in her mouth, 'it's still a few hours until Early-Eve. While we're waiting, let's go out. I heard that the guy you fancy is playing at Club Abraxas. Markes, isn't it?'

'I don't fancy him,' said Retra quickly.

Suki scraped the last of her bacon through her sauce. 'Yeah, right.'

nine

The Abraxas line ran downhill from Vank; a weaving, rocking trip that gave Retra time to stare out of the window at the mountainside's brilliant nightscape while Suki's prattle became faster and more excited.

They'd gone to confession before leaving Vank but Test had been dispensing and hadn't forced Retra to ingest the pod. Afterwards she'd dropped hers over the edge of the platform as they got on the kar.

'You have to take it,' Suki warned, as she swallowed a whole red bead. 'They'll know.'

'I don't like them. They made me see things – visions.'

'What-kinda-visions?'

'Demons.'

Suki pulled a face. Then she giggled. 'It-made-you-dance-all-sexy,' she said.

Retra noticed that most of the people in the kar were speaking in the same kind of high-pitched, jerky voices as Suki. Had she sounded the same?

When the kar stopped, they piled out, pushing and shoving and mock-arguing. Retra searched the faces on the platform, looking for her brother, but she saw no one that could be him.

She and Suki followed the crowd as they walked the lamp-lit path to Club Abraxas.

Unlike the Drop, which they'd accessed from a bridge, the Club Abraxas entry was deep in the hillside.

As they walked along, the warm air played over Retra like a wet tongue, making her skin pimple.

'*Want you,*' a voice whispered from the dark. '*Soon.*'

Retra glanced to either side of the path but saw nothing save shadowy, low bushes, stretching away into the night. The smell of musk made her look up into the sky. The black rainbow of bats was back, cutting through the starlight in a long arc of black.

'Suki, do you hear that?'

'What?-Hear-what?-What're-you-talking-about?-All-I-can-smell-is-stinking-bats-Can't-hear-nothing-'cept-my-own-heartbeat-bang-bang-bang,' Suki raved. She jigged as they walked, unable to keep her limbs still.

Retra pressed closer to the people in front of her. She felt relieved when the stars blinked out and they entered Abraxas's cave system.

The first cave was small, more like an entrance hall, with Ripers standing around watching new arrivals.

She and Suki passed through it quickly into the next, which was wider with a raised stage cut from the rock wall, and passages running off it in different directions. A band of musicians spread across the stage, tuning instruments, most of which Retra didn't recognise.

'Krissie-says-Abraxas-has-performers-in-all-its-caves-We-just-have-to-find-the-one-with-Markes-now.'

Suki's fast talking unnerved Retra. So did her jerky movements.

'We could look separately,' she said, feeling the sudden need to get some distance from Suki's glittering eyes and fast mouth.

Suki danced on her toes a little, agitated. Tears filled her eyes and she ran off without a word.

Retra went to follow after her but fingers gripped her wrist and swung her around.

Modai.

'In a hurry, baby bat? Why is that?' He curled back his lips to show off sharp teeth. 'What did you see? *Who* did you see?'

Two more Ripers joined him. Retra recognised Forlorn as one of them, but not the other. They crowded around her, blocking out most of the light from the club. She tried to squeeze between them but Modai caught her wrist again and held it, crushing the bones.

Retra made herself think outside the pain, the way she'd practised in Grave. She had survived the agony of the obedience strip where others had died from it. So could she think through this. 'No one.'

'Why were you running?'

'Is there a rule not to run?' she asked.

'The rule is not to keep things from us.'

She held his dead gaze with one of her own. She would tell him nothing.

'You've caused trouble among the Guardians,' hissed Modai. 'I knew you needed to be watched. Tell me what you are doing or –' He lifted his other hand as if to strike her.

Retra twisted away, feeling his fingernails scratching her skin as she wrenched her wrist from his fingers.

She ran towards one of the passages but somehow the Ripers were in front of her before she could reach it. How could humans move so fast?

Retra glanced behind her to the crowd collected on the dance floor. The Ripers' movements had caught their attention and they stopped dancing as a tall figure cut through the middle of them.

'Modai?'

The Riper stepped back, head bowed in immediate obedience. 'Lenoir.'

'What has this batling done that you seek to harry her?'

'I sense her falseness.'

'Has she broken any of our rules?'

'No, Lenoir.'

'Then I suggest you and Leyste find other amusements.' Lenoir's voice was soft, almost gentle, and yet Modai became rigid.

Leyste? Retra searched the face of the unknown Riper – was he Leyste? Why did Leyste and Modai wish to taunt her?

She glanced back at Lenoir but he continued to stare at Modai.

Both of them had pale skin, dark, straight hair and lean, muscular physiques. How was it that on Lenoir the combination was so magnificent, and yet on Modai it was repellent?

'Hey there! Sorry, did I interrupt something?' A body barrelled into the middle of the group, breaking the tension.

It was Rollo. His red hair was dyed black and plastered to his head with sweat; his bare chest covered with snaking tattoos. He grinned and grabbed Retra around the waist, planting a wet kiss on her lips. 'Been looking everywhere for you.'

Retra stiffened but didn't move. Rollo felt hot and damp, his skin slippery against her bare arm and neck. His breath smelt sweet like her father's, after prayer meetings and prayer wine, when he came to her room and spoke in maudlin tones of his disappointment in his son, and his marrow-deep conviction that she would not be allowed to follow the same path. *Stay pure, Retra*, Father had said, over and over. *Stay pure.*

But Charlonge's warning chafed against her father's, as if one sought to rub the other out. *Modesty is a sin in Ixion.*

She leaned into Rollo's arms, pretending to welcome his affection. 'M-me too,' she stammered. 'Where were you?'

Modai gazed at them with suspicion.

'Come on,' Rollo said. He began to steer her away from the Ripers towards one of the passages.

Retra felt Lenoir's gaze follow her.

'What did they want?' asked Rollo, when they entered the next cave.

'Nothing. I mean, I was running.'

'So what?'

Retra shrugged. 'Modai wanted to know why. I wouldn't tell him. I didn't think I should ... have to.'

'Stubborn, huh? Most people would tell Modai anything he asked. He's so frossin' scary.'

They walked over to a dark nook furnished with low couches. Couples huddled together on the seats, some kissing, others more than kissing, hands roaming each other's bodies.

Retra wanted to turn away from it but walking in the near dark required concentration.

Rollo crooked his head against hers, clamping her body against him. 'Don't look behind but Modai's followed us,' he whispered.

They walked, entwined to an empty couch where Rollo fell onto the plush seat, pulling her down with him.

Modai stood at the cave entrance, watching.

Retra slid closer to Rollo and he put his arm around her again. They looked like any of the other couples there, she told herself. She tilted her face up to look at him and he pulled a face at her.

'I saw you come in but I was kinda annoyed at how you ran off on me at the re-birth, so I was going to ignore you,' said Rollo with disarming honesty. 'Then I saw Modai hassling you.'

'You know him?'

He rolled his eyes and licked a bead of sweat from his upper lip. 'Everyone does. They say he's the one who makes you disappear if you're a troublemaker. But he seems real interested in you. Even back at the Register he was.'

'You noticed?'

'I notice a lot.'

Neither of them said anything more for a moment or two, letting the dance drumbeat fill the gap.

'You're here looking for someone, aren't you? I mean like ... someone who came before you,' Rollo said, breaking their silence.

Her eyes widened in surprise.

He shrugged and frowned. "S obvious you don't really wanna be here. You're a Seal, and not the rebel type Seal who wants to run away. You're way too tight and rigid. And you're not looking for this ...' He stroked her face.

She flinched.

'See,' he said.

'It's not that I don't want ...' she protested. 'It's just that ... you didn't ask and I ... I ...' She let the words fade. How could she tell him she found him unappealing?

Conversation lapsed between them again.

Rollo stared openly at the couple making out across from them, his expression envious. Retra thought about getting up and leaving but Modai still lingered at the railing near the lift.

'What if I tell you about me? Will you trust me a bit more? I mean ... I'm making most of the conversation anyway, I might as well.' Rollo laughed then, just as easily he had frowned before. 'I ran away from home.'

Retra stared at him. 'We all did that.'

'No ... I ran away *from* home. Not *to* Ixion. See ... my dad is ... he's on the Grave Council.'

Retra swallowed to wet a sudden dry patch in the back of her throat. *A councillor's son.* She'd never met one before. Council lived in the wealthy part of Grave North, in rich houses behind the giant, growing wall that protected them from ... everything. Not like the grim mesh fence of the Seal Enclave. No wonder Rollo knew so much about history. Councillors were allowed free reign of the library. They decided on what people learned. They made Grave's rules. The Council had ordered the warden to keep surveillance on her family. 'I d-don't understand. Why did you leave then?'

'He wanted me to be a councillor too. It usually works that way. Father to son.' Rollo screwed up his face as if he was nursing a mouthful of bitters. 'I hate what they do. My dad took me to court sessions to prepare me – all these creepy old men in wigs and masks. Making rules. Making people's lives a misery. Telling what they can and can't do. How they should think.'

'Hush,' whispered Retra, automatically. 'Don't speak of them like that.'

The air squashed from her lungs at the memory of the Council's clicking electro-eyes on her nakedness.

'Why? They can't do anything to us here –' Rollo broke off in sudden understanding. 'You've been on probation, haven't you?'

Retra crossed her arms over her chest in an involuntary movement.

'See. *You* must understand. That's why I don't want to be one of them. They have no right to do that sort of thing. No right!' he cried out.

Retra wished that he would go away. His vehemence frightened her, and his careless talk. He didn't seem scared of anyone and she thought him foolish to be that way. He was like Joel. So confident and sure of what he thought. *Why can't I be like that? Why must I over-think and be so careful?*

And yet, she'd attacked Brand when her anger had taken over. Perhaps she was not so different to Joel? Perhaps she was changing? 'I hit a Riper,' she said to him. 'She was touching a girl called Krista-belle and I ... picked up a stool and ...'

Rollo's eyes widened. 'You're the one who smashed the Riper with a chair? Everyone's talking about it, but I didn't believe it. What happened?'

'Lenoir came and stopped Brand before she could punish me. But I don't think it's over. Modai said I'd caused trouble among them.'

'Why did you get involved? That's not a Seal thing to do.'

'I ... what Brand was doing to Krista-belle ... she was scared ... like when the warden gave me the obedience strip.'

'You had a pain strip? Fross! How did you leave the compound then?'

Retra gave him a small, anxious smile. 'I practised. The pain.'

Rollo's expression changed. His eyes widened in a kind of admiration and he enveloped her in a comforting hug.

But Retra didn't want comfort right now. She wanted to leave.

As she tried to edge out his grip he held on. 'There's something I'm going to tell you. The real reason that I came here,' he said.

'What's that?'

'You can't tell anyone this. Not yet. Not until I say. Promise.'

She nodded, hesitantly, not sure that she wanted to know Rollo's secrets.

'When I went to the Grave Council meetings I got to know things. I listened to how they talked. They made lots of loud, empty noise most of the time but when they wanted something, their voices changed. Each time they talked of Ixion – how depraved the place was and what they could do to stop us coming here – their voices were loud and empty. At first I didn't think much about it. Then one night when

Father and I were walking home with Councillor Jarvis and Councillor Mison, someone called to them from the shadows. My father hustled me away but I saw who it was.'

Retra waited.

Rollo's stare grew intent, as though he was trying to force the memory to life before them. 'It was a Riper. At least that's what I thought he was. I had to come here to be sure.'

'That can't be.'

'It is! I saw Modai there,' he said hotly. 'And now I know that the emptiness in the councillors' voices was real. They pretend to be angry about Ixion – but they aren't, not really. It's a game.'

'What do you mean – a game?'

'I don't know but I've come here to find out why the Ripers are visiting Grave. There's some tie between the two places that nobody knows about. I plan to tell the Youth Circle about it.'

'What can they do?' Retra felt suddenly exhausted, as if the energy that she'd gained from *petite nuit* had burned through her already.

'They're the ones who represent us to the Guardians. They're specially chosen, and they get extra privileges for it. Look, there's one of them there.'

Retra followed the line of Rollo's pointed finger to a guy sharing a single armchair seat with a girl. He looked much the same as anyone.

'They have a circle tattoo on their temples.'

In the dim light it was hard to see, but Retra had noticed circles on others. 'What sort of privileges do they get?'

Rollo shrugged. 'Not sure exactly except that they get to go everywhere except the forbidden places, and they don't need to rest as much as we do.'

'Don't they burn out quickly then?'

''parently not. Ripers tweak their adrenal glands to give 'em extra time with no deficit. But they have to pledge their service to Ixion.'

'What does *that* mean?'

'Being good citizens. Not like the gangers. Telling the Ripers if they see people breaking the rules.'

'If they serve the Ripers then how will they help you?'

He shook his head glumly. 'I don't know. Who else is there to go to?'

Retra didn't know what to say to him. 'When will you tell them?'

'Soon. I wanted to find my way around before I open my mouth.' He grinned, cheering up. 'I'm loud but I'm not stupid. Will you come with me to the Circle? You can tell them about how things are for you in Grave; how evil the Council are.'

'Perhaps,' said Retra. Kero and Krista-belle hadn't sounded impressed by the Youth Circle. 'But not now, I have somewhere else to go.'

'Another club?'

'No.' Should she tell Rollo what she was doing? He'd seen something important in Grave. Maybe he should come with her; learn more about Ixion before he went to the Youth Council. 'It's a meeting. I've been invited to become a member of the White Wings.'

'You! In a gang?' Rollo made no effort to hide his astonishment and disbelief.

'You've heard of them?'

'I've been resting at Goa. Place stinks of mould, and there're vines growing in through the cracks in the walls: giant roaches come in on them. Or so someone said. I couldn't relax, waiting for one to land on my face. Anyway, that's where the Wings mainly hang out. They're way cool. Especially Kero. Word is he can take anyone in a fight except for Dark Eve from the Cursed League.'

'I wouldn't know about –'

'Take me to the meeting!'

Retra felt uncomfortable. 'I'm not sure –'

'Why not?' Rollo gave her a wounded look. 'I told you about the Council and the Ripers.'

'It's just that …' She started to defend herself but trailed off when she saw his gaze drift across her shoulder and his eyes grow wider.

'Look at those *hot* pants,' Rollo gasped.

Suki was standing behind Retra, alone, pretending not to see them.

'That's Suki.'

'You know her?'

Retra nodded.

'Well, for Grave's sake, Retra, introduce me!'

ten

Retra got up and went over to Suki with Rollo at her heels. Suki tried to turn away but Retra stepped around in front of her. 'It can't be long until Early-Eve. We should go to the meeting now.'

'Oh-you-still-want-me-to-come-do-you?'

'Yes, I do,' said Retra. 'But the bead you took is making you agitated.'

A relieved smile spread across Suki's face. She scratched her skin. 'Dunno what that means but it's making me itchy.'

'What colour bead did you have?' piped in Rollo.

'The-red-one-who-are-you?'

'I'm Rollo. Retra and I go way back.'

'We do no –'

But Rollo cut across her. 'The red ones are usually okay, but some people react more to them. It's the black ones that are really strong. You don't want to take them. Phew!' He tapped his head. 'Like a bomb's gone off in your scone. Now, where's this meeting?'

Suki gave her fiercest stare, which came off a little weird as she hopped from one foot to the other and scratched her arms. 'What's-it-to-you?'

'Like I said, Retra and I are buddies, and I'm thinking of joining the Wings as well.'

Retra was dumbfounded by Rollo's easy twist of the truth.

'So you know where the Grotto is then?' said Suki before Retra could stop her.

Rollo gave Retra a victory smile. 'Sure. Down the mountain from Illi. You have to go back to Vank station and switch kars. I can show you.'

Retra glanced around, carefully. Modai had moved a little closer to them. Perhaps it was better have Rollo with them. He seemed to have an instinct for handling situations. 'Modai is still watching us. Suki and I'll go first. You should wait a few moments. Look bored, and then leave. We'll wait for you on the Vank platform.'

Rollo nodded in approval. 'Sounds like a plan. Make sure you wait. You won't find the Grotto without me.'

'What's-going-on?' asked Suki. 'Why is Modai watching?'

'He's been watching Retra since we came through the Register together,' Rollo said. 'He hassled her just a little while ago. I saw it and distracted them. He says she's caused trouble among the Guardians.'

Retra winced at the totally unguarded way Rollo spoke. As if the three of them were confidantes when they'd only just met.

'What?' he said, sensing her reaction. 'That's the truth, isn't it?'

'It's-okay-she's-not-used-to-talking-to-people-It's-the-Seal-thing.' Suki linked arms with Retra. 'Come-on-silent-Seal. Let's-go.'

Surprisingly, Suki's teasing didn't offend her and she was smiling when they ran into Markes and Cal in the foyer. They were with a boy who had circles tattooed on his temples.

'Retra?' Markes looked her up and down. 'You look different.'

Retra thought he did too, but didn't say so. He wore fitted black pants and a thin white T-shirt that showed off his broad chest and strong arms. His guitar was slung over his shoulder. At least he wasn't speaking quickly like Suki.

'Hello, Markes.'

'You're not leaving yet, are you? I'll be playing soon. Ruin has come to listen. You should stay.'

The boy with the circle tattoos put out his hand. Something about his milky-blue eyes made Retra uncomfortable. 'Hello, Retra, and ...'

'Suki,' said Suki. 'We-can't-stay-we've-got-something-important-to-go-to.'

Retra squeezed Suki's wrist in warning, but it was too late. Ruin's attention was caught. So was Cal's. She flicked her straight white hair back from her face and stared hard at Retra.

'Hey, Seal, I heard you upset the Ripers already. Good effort.'

'She-was-protecting-one-of-us,' said Suki.

'Whatever. What's so important that *you'd* miss Markes play? More trouble?' asked Cal, provocatively.

'Mind-your-business.' Suki scowled at Cal. Her almond eyes narrowed to angry slits.

Retra tried to think of something to allay Ruin's curious look. 'We're meeting some boys at another club. That's all,' she said.

'Okay. See you later then.' Markes seemed disappointed.

'Yes,' said Retra. She wanted to take him aside and explain but it was too risky. He might tell Cal. Or worse, Ruin. From what Rollo had said, the Youth Circle didn't approve of the gangs at all. She took Suki's arm and drew her on.

'What *is* her problem?' snarled Suki.

'Her name is Cal,' said Retra. 'Don't look back.'

They hurried back along the path to the station. This time nothing spoke to Retra from the dark. Still, she was shivering despite the sticky warmth when they boarded the kar.

'What's wrong?' asked Suki, as they took one of the back seats.

Retra didn't answer her even though Suki's voice sounded more normal and she'd stopped scratching.

'Look,' Suki said, after a while. 'Friends talk to each other. That's what they do. Tell each other things.'

Retra licked her lips and forced herself to speak. 'Do they?'

'Haven't you ever had a friend?'

Retra stared out the window. Joel was her friend. Did that count? And Toola had been for short while, though Retra knew her real interest had been in Joel.

But Suki wouldn't let it go. 'You've *never* had a friend? That's impossible.'

'There was a girl called Toola, but after my brother left and the warden came to live with us she stopped ...'

'What? Being your friend?' Suki frowned. 'I don't really understand your world but not everyone from Grave is as private as you. Look at Rollo. He's not like that. What's it like there?'

Retra leaned back on the seat. She'd only ever *thought* about her world, never spoken of it to another person. Perhaps she could tell Suki. *The Council can't hear me now*, she reminded herself. *The warden can't touch me.*

'Seal South is stricter than the rest of Grave. We aren't allowed to speak to others at will. Only at certain times.'

'That's just plain loco,' said Suki.

'We're taught that our Elders left the Old World to found a better place with stronger morals. The Old World had become depraved and without rules. The young were vicious and selfish and self-destructive. The Elders called their behaviour a sickness.' As she spoke, the memory of her history lessons flooded back. 'They sailed among the stars looking for the perfect place to start again but their travelling ship malfunctioned and they were forced to make their home on this world. They built Grave, and sealed it off from the native barbarians who shared the land with them. Growing walls kept the barbarians out, and over time they gave up trying to fight us and left us alone.' Retra stopped, eyes widening. 'I always thought that part was just a story. But now I see that there are other cultures on Grave. Maybe your people are the barbarians?'

Suki crossed her arms. 'Well, for a start, this world is not called Grave. It's called Stra'ha'ine. And your people sound like barbarians, not mine.'

'I suppose so,' allowed Retra, not wanting to upset the girl.

'You mean, "I *guess* so"?'

They both smiled and the awkward moment passed.

Retra continued with her story. 'Some of the Elders believed in firmer rules than the others. They moved to the south of the city and put up their own walls. They called them the Sealed South Walls. That's where I'm from. That's how we got the name.'

'So what's it like in Seal South?'

'Cold,' she said. *In so many ways.*

'What about your parents?'

'They believe in the rules. Especially my father. Mother does as he tells her. She used to read to me but he told her to stop. She used to brush my hair out at night but he said it encouraged unclean thoughts.'

'*Unclean thoughts.*' Suki smirked. 'Why wouldn't you want them, anyway?'

But Retra was too caught in her memories to react to Suki's teasing. 'After my brother left, Mother didn't speak much. It was as if all the life went out of her.'

Suki screwed up her nose. 'Your home sucks. Mine was just boring. Hunt, kill, skin, salt, cook, eat, clean and bury. Then start all over again. But we laugh a lot.'

'What about Liam?'

'Won't be the end of the world if he doesn't come here. I mean, that Rollo's kind of cute.'

Retra didn't know what to say to that, so she didn't say anything.

When Rollo arrived at Vank the three caught the next kar on the Illi line. He sat in front of them and hung over the seat the way Krista-belle had done before, chattering to Suki about Goa and the White Wings, while the kar creaked along its cables like a tired beast.

Retra stared out, noticing how Ixion's lights seemed a little dimmer and the dark seemed lighter. This must be what Kero meant by Early-Eve.

'What causes the ever-night?' she asked, interrupting them.

Rollo stopped short and stared at her. 'The anomaly, of course.'

'What in Stra' is an anomaly? asked Suki.

'The Golden Spiral. When we crossed into it on the barge, the dark came. It's some kind of disturbance in the normal way of things. The Grave Council have been studying it for years without an answer, so they call it an anomaly. It's just another name for something abnormal.'

'In Stra'ha we call it the Blur. Have you ever had spots floating across your eyes when you stared at the sky?'

Rollo nodded.

'It's like one of those. A dark spot in front of what you see,' she said.

'Does that mean it's everlasting?' Retra wanted to know.

'Who cares?' said Suki. 'It's not like we'll be here forever. One day we'll be withdrawn to another place.'

Retra hunched her shoulders at that and stared back out the window. She would be gone before then.

eleven

The Illi platform was wider than Vank and lit by ornate iron and glass lamps. A cobbled path branched out from the wooden platform along the mountainside. Rollo led the way, walking backwards along the cobblestones so that he could talk. Retra stayed close to Suki, wary of what lingered beyond the path. She could smell the electricity of the dark, feel its charged fingers reaching for her.

'We're here,' said Rollo.

Retra lifted her gaze. Uphill from the steps stood the vast stone edifice of Illi church. Where Vank was spire-angular and ornamented inside and out with hardened wood, Illi was built on rounded lines and decorated by bevelled mantles and pillars. Fire torches lit the outside and, as the warm breeze played with their light, they splashed grotesque shadows across the face of the church.

Rollo pointed downwards. 'The Grotto is at the bottom of these steps. It's part of the old Illi gardens and was an outside place to worship. I haven't been down there yet. At Goa, they told me that the Grotto isn't safe. People go missing from the steps all the time.'

'I can't see any lights,' said Suki. She was alive with curiosity. 'Do you think anyone is down there?'

'There's a rock wall at the bottom of the steps. It curves like a half-moon. The Grotto is on the other side of it. The wall will most likely shield any lights. I guess that's why people go there. It's private.'

Retra stared at the steps disappearing down into the night. 'It's getting darker again.' Even as they stood there, the lights of Illi grew brighter, signalling the passing of Early-Eve. 'We should hurry.'

'Me first!' said Suki, as she went to plunge down the steps.

Retra caught her arm. 'Wait, there's a password to get in.'

'What is it?' asked Rollo.

'The age of rage,' Retra whispered to them.

Suki pulled away and kept moving. 'Still gonna be first!'

'Hey, wait!' Rollo catapulted after her.

Retra followed them more slowly, heart in mouth. A dull glow lit the rough steps as if somehow it produced its own energy. Even so, shadows seemed closer than they should be. Was this really the right place? Did Rollo know or was he making it up? She found it hard to trust someone she hardly knew. And yet he'd trusted her.

Retra's doubts grew stronger than her conviction as she continued down. Several times she thought about turning back.

She heard scraping sounds on one side of steps.

Like you. Smell good.

She pressed her hands to her ears.

Mine. The voice stayed insistent and clear.

A scream climbed into the back of her throat and caught there, robbing her lungs of their passage of air. She looked below for Rollo and Suki but they'd disappeared at the bottom of the steps, perhaps to the other side of the wall.

She should run back to Illi. Or the station. But what if Joel was down there? What if her brother was this close?

Come to me.

She made a noise, a harsh, frightened sound that cleared her throat. Air flowed back into her tight chest and she began to run downward. *Don't fall. Don't fall. Don't fall.*

Invisible fingers grabbed at her ankles but she lifted her knees high, touching only her toes onto the stonework. Hot breath caressed her neck, and soft touches like clammy kisses fell on her arms. She flailed, not sure if she imagined them or not.

Joel. Joel. Be there. Please be there.

The steps ended abruptly, a wall looming from the dark without warning. Her hands slammed into rock, jarring all the way to her shoulders. Her desperate fingers grasped the cool iron loop of a door latch. She twisted it with all her strength but it didn't budge. She let go and beat at the door with her fists.

'The age of rage,' she cried. 'The age of rage.'

The heavy door swung inward. She stumbled through it, past tall boys armed with pointed sticks, into Rollo's waiting arms.

'What took you so long?' His grin was eerie and distorted by the glow of hundreds of candle lamps.

'You left me,' Retra gasped.

'Sssh,' said Suki. 'They're starting.'

Retra pulled away from Rollo and gazed down into the Grotto. The candle lamps illuminated a hundred or more gangers, sitting in loose formation on the rock floor of what seemed to be a cave without its roof. The walls were dotted with hollows that contained statues – many of them ruined. Retra recognised one as a dolmen – the three upright stones of a burial chamber that the Grave Elders wore embroidered on their formal gowns.

Exotic, pale flowers on creepers clung to sections of the rock wall, exuding their pale beauty and sweet scent into the air, and lending the Grotto an ethereal look.

'What are they?' breathed Retra.

'Moonflowers,' said Suki. 'They only come out at night.'

'I've never seen them before.'

'Probably too cold where you come from. They like warmth. We get them down the mountain in Stra'ha. But only in summer.'

Retra wanted to touch one, inhale its perfume, but the crowd below them began clapping.

'I have to get closer,' Retra whispered to Suki.

The girl nodded. 'Over there.' She pointed. 'More steps.'

The three walked around the ledge and climbed down the steps to stand just above the back row. The White Wings were in front of them, their heads wrapped in bandanas. To their left sat a group wearing spikes around their throats and wrists.

'That's the Freeks,' said Rollo. 'They look like a bunch of pen quills.'

Suki stifled a giggle. 'What about the ones with white cloaks?'

'They're the Ghosts. Their cloaks are made of old ghost bat skins. They collect the dead ones and sew them together. Some of them even leave the heads on.'

'Who are the others?' asked Retra. The group who sat opposite the White Wings wore ordinary dance clothes like her and Suki and Rollo, except for the very front row. Those sitting there wore hard leather tunics and pants that resembled armour that Retra had seen in history archivolos.

'That's gotta be the League,' said Suki.

'I don't understand how they get those clothes. Mine are waiting for me in my locker.'

'That's 'cos we're newbies,' said Rollo. 'Those that have been here a while swap gear around. Trade. And most of the time the Leaguers dress normally. Only their important members wear the leathers full time.'

'How come you know so much?' Suki gave him a suspicious stare.

'What've you been doing since you got here?' asked Rollo.

Suki shrugged. 'Going to the clubs. Watching out for her.' She nodded at Retra. 'Why?'

'I've been talking to people. Asking questions. And now I've got one for you. What in the fross is going on here?'

'Krista-belle from the Wings isn't the only one Brand's touched,' said Retra suddenly.

'Brand? Is she the one you hammered? The scar lady?'

Retra nodded. She was listening to him, but her eyes flew from face to face searching for Joel. *Where are you? Where?*

At the centre of the Grotto, where the gangs faced each other, stood four figures. Retra recognised Kero but not the others. Two of them were like him, thickset young guys with confident postures, one wearing a spiked choker and wrist bands, the other in a stiff white cloak. The fourth caught Retra's full attention – a tall, broad-shouldered girl with a huge sword in her hand. She towered over the rest.

'That must be Dark Eve,' said Rollo. His voice echoed the same awe that Retra felt. Dark Eve was imposing in size, but it was more than that. Energy seemed to crackle around her.

Kero held up his hand to the assembled. 'Quiet!'

The single word carried effortlessly around the rocky amphitheatre, and the crowd quieted. He beckoned to someone by his feet.

Krista-belle stood up and bowed to the crowd. Her hair was piled high, and even from the back of the Grotto, Retra could see the sweep of heavy eye shadow from her eyelids to her temple. She wore her white bandana around her neck like a necklace, above a tight, black shift and chunky heels.

Kero took her hand and held it in his, as he addressed everyone. 'Krista-belle has a story. Listen to it.'

His girlfriend slipped her hand free of his and walked slowly around the four in the circle, gathering the attention of all the gangs.

When she was sure they were listening, she spoke. 'One string ago, at the Drop, Brand tried to take me. I was on a rest couch and the bitch-Riper fell on me. She grabbed me.' Krista-belle touched her breasts and ran her hand down between her legs. 'She stuck her tongue places, and her hands. She bit my neck. I wanted to puke but I couldn't move.'

'What happened?' shouted someone.

'A newbie saw her and smashed a stool into her.'

A roar of approval went up.

'Which newbie?' a few of them wanted to know, when the crowd quieted again.

'A Seal,' said Krista-belle. 'A girl. And that's all I'm saying.'

'Hey, that's you,' said Rollo, digging Retra in the side. 'You're a hero.'

The Wings sitting in front of them turned around and looked. They started whispering to each other.

'Sssh,' Retra told Rollo. 'Listen.'

'Point is,' added Kero now, 'Brand's dangerous. Krissie's not the only one she's touched.'

The Ghost's leader spoke next. 'One of ours, Amora, disappeared six strings ago. She was last seen at Bella Death, talking to Brand.'

'The Ripers are our Guardians. This shouldn't be happening,' added the leader of the Freeks.

Murmurs started up.

'What do we do?' someone shouted.

'We should bring the Youth Circle here,' said the Ghosts' leader. 'Tell them what we know.'

'No! They're spies for the Ripers,' said Kero. 'We – the Wings – think we should post guards on the paths outside the clubs. Look after our own people.'

'The Freeks support the Wings on this,' said the Freeks' leader.

Kero turned to the armour-clad girl who'd been silent throughout. 'Where does the League stand?'

Dark Eve took her time answering, walking in a slow circle around the others, the way Krista-belle had. When she did speak, the Grotto fell absolutely silent. 'Your plan is selfish. The ideas are narrow. What about those who don't belong to the Wings or the League, Ghosts or Freeks? Plenty don't. Who'll look out for them?'

'That's their problem,' said Kero. 'Let 'em take care of themselves. Make their own way.'

A cheer rose among the Wings.

'The League believes the Guardians should answer to all of us,' thundered Dark Eve. 'They use the Youth Circle to spy. Not represent. The League supports Ruzalia. She knows the Guardians for what they really are and she sends us a warning. Stand up to them, she says. Fight them. Take this place for ourselves.'

The Leaguers and a spattering of others cat-called in support, but just as many booed and hissed.

'A lot would follow her, I reckon,' whispered Suki. 'She acts like a true soldier.'

Retra glanced at Rollo. His face shone with excitement in the candlelight and his breathing came quickly as if he'd been running.

'What is it?' she asked him.

'I should tell *her* about the Council,' he said. 'Not the Youth Circle.'

'What Council?' asked Suki.

Retra stared at Rollo. She shook her head imperceptibly at him. Rollo's information was dangerous. The less people who knew, the better.

'We should vote,' Kero insisted, drawing their attention back to the centre of the Grotto. 'Who believes we should protect our own?'

All the Wings and the Ghosts raised their hands.

'Who thinks we should fight the Ripers?'

The League all stood, but the Freeks were divided. Some raised their hands but others didn't vote, bringing the weight of the vote down on Kero's side.

His satisfaction was plain. 'Majority says we protect our own. Meeting's done.'

'Which one's the Seal? We want to know,' hollered some Freeks down near the front.

One of the Wings sitting in front of Retra stood up. 'Here. She's right here!' He turned and pointed.

A hundred or more curious stares fell upon her. Retra was overwhelmed by the attention and her legs started to buckle.

But Suki held her firm and pinched the skin on her wrist. 'Be proud of it.'

On her other side, Rollo pointed and preened, making silly 'I'm with her' gestures. If her legs had been able to move she would have kicked him.

Instead, she clung to Suki's words and dug down for the Seal-trained strength within her. Her back straightened and her shoulders squared. She kept her face as expressionless as she could manage.

The crowd began to clap. Then everyone was on their feet, swarming towards her. Bat-skin capes scraped against her arms, and many hands slapped her back in congratulations.

'Good job, Seal.'

'On ya.'

'Brilliant.'

'Wow. Brave work.'

The accolades blurred into a stream of noise but Retra was only aware of one thing; Dark Eve staring up at her, frowning.

Then shouts erupted behind them all.

'Ripers!' cried the sentry guards. 'Ripers coming from Illi.'

The clapping ceased and the crowd stampeded up the stairs through the gate.

As the Grotto emptied, Retra moved with them, twisting and turning to catch better angles of their faces.

Joel, where are you? Joel?

Her gaze tracked back and forth. Dark Eve stood out among them all, taller than anyone else, more striking. But it was the figure next to her that sent Retra's pulse racing; something deeply familiar in his posture.

She started to run towards him but he'd gone through the amphitheatre gate before she could take more than a few steps. Then Kero and Krista-belle were beside her, racing up behind the last of the Wings.

'Hurry up.' Krista-belle grabbed her shoulders and turned her around. '*You* of all people don't wanna be caught down here. Kero and I know another way out.'

'What about Suki?'

'She's up there, with some guy.' Kero pointed to the ledge at the top of the stairs.

'That's Rollo.' Should she say friend?

Kero motioned up to Suki for them to wait. When they reached them, Kero didn't waste time explaining. 'This way,' he said.

He headed along the ledge in the opposite direction to the gate until they reached the far edge of the Grotto wall where the dolmen Retra had seen before stood embedded in its own tiny hollow. Next to it was a swathe of moonflowers. Kero lifted the curtain of creeper aside and stepped behind it. Krista-belle followed him, beckoning the others.

Suki went next.

When Retra stepped in behind her, she found herself in a low, dark tunnel that slanted upward.

Rollo bumped into her, as she waited for her eyes to adjust to the even lower light, pushing her against Suki.

'Legendary,' said Suki. 'Where does this go?'

'It's a bit of a climb but it connects with the paths just beneath Illi,' said Kero.

Retra touched the stone wall. 'It's ancient. And well built.'

'There's a few of them around, linking places. I only know of a couple. Dark Eve probably knows more. They must have built them so that the monks could keep out of the weather, back when Ixion had sunlight.'

'Did it ever?' asked Rollo.

'Depends on which story you believe,' said Kero. 'Let's go.'

They climbed in silence, saving their breath for the ascent. The walls were as moist and close as a wet glove. Retra wanted to ask Kero about the night creatures but feared to mention them aloud in this place. What if the voice she'd heard on the Illi steps was near? What if it could see her?

Something grabbed her ankle and she bit off a scream.

'Sorry,' apologised Rollo. 'I slipped.'

'This tunnel is eerie,' said Retra.

Rollo grunted. 'Try being last in line. I keep hearing voices, and feeling things crawling on my skin.'

'Oh my braveheart,' Suki carolled from in front.

'Leave him alone, Suki,' said Retra. 'I can feel things too.'

'Shh!' Kero called back to them. 'The Ripers'll hear you.'

No one spoke again until they emerged onto a narrow Lesser Path, just below Illi. Kero made them wait inside the remnants of the ruined prayer hutch that hid the entrance to the tunnel until he'd checked that the steps were clear.

'Come on,' he called.

They piled out of the hutch and hurried upwards to the Greater Path.

Krista-belle and Suki burst into giggles of relief when they finally reached the Illi platform. Rollo danced around in front of them, entertaining the others already waiting for the next kar.

A couple wearing bat-skin coats approached Retra.

'Cool stuff that you did,' one of them said.

Retra didn't know what to say, so she nodded. Her heart still beat wildly from the climb and their run to the platform.

A kar arrived, and the couple got on first. Retra and the others followed, taking two seats between the five of them. Retra squeezed in with Krista-belle and Kero.

Krista-belle grinned at her. 'You're famous.'

'Did you see the guy you're looking for in the Grotto?' asked Kero.

She shook her head, not ready to tell them that she thought he'd been with Dark Eve. 'You won the vote.'

'Yeah,' he said quietly. 'But Dark Eve won't give up. She'll keep doing what she wants, making the Ripers angry. Then they'll take it out on us.'

'Is that what Brand's doing? Is she taking revenge on us because the League is helping the over-agers?' whispered Retra.

'Maybe.' He slipped his arm around Krista-belle and pulled her close to him. 'But the Riper-bitch won't ever get a chance to get near you again.'

'Aww,' said Krista-belle softly. She nuzzled into his neck.

Retra looked away from them.

'Where do the League spend their time?' she asked Kero when the pair pulled apart again.

'Ravens. It's a club on the end of the Los Fien line. The Lesser Paths around there are well lit. They practise their combat out there.'

Combat. Retra's stomach hardened at the thought. 'Ravens. I think I'd like to go there.'

Kero and Krista-belle looked at each other and nodded. 'Sure. Music's good.'

Retra tapped Suki on the shoulder. She and Rollo were sitting close together in front of them. Almost as close as Krista-belle and Kero.

'What now, my hero?' teased Suki, half turning.

'Party time at Ravens,' said Krista-belle.

Suki rubbed her hands together. *'Beko.'*

They all stared at her.

'It's Stra'hine,' she said. 'It means time to celebrate.'

'Beko,' said Rollo. He threw his hands in the air and wiggled his shoulders. 'Let's go *beko.*'

twelve

The entrance to Ravens was similar to the Drop – across a bridge from the kar platform straight into the club. The Ravens' bridge, though, led into the bottom floor rather than the top.

'How do you get to the Lesser Paths?' Retra asked Kero as they climbed a wide, sweeping staircase that reminded Retra of a bird's wing.

'You don't. Not from the bridge. Ravens has back doors. Not all the clubs do. I guess they were all built at different times. That's probably why Eve likes it here best. More than one escape route.'

'Escape route?'

He turned to Retra, his eyes narrowing. 'She's in hiding from the Ripers. Others from the League feed her, bring her clothes. She survives outside "normal" means.' He wiggled his fingers in the air to emphasise normal.

'Can't the Ripers just alter her metabolism like they did to ours? Make her burn out quickly?'

'They'd have to catch her first. She's pretty good at hiding. Doesn't take her *petite nuit* in the churches. Only comes to the clubs occasionally. Most of the times she's on the Lesser Paths, out of sight. Or in the tunnels.'

'What about the Grotto?'

'It was risky for her to come to the meet. If the Ripers had caught up with us ... but knowing Eve, she had an escape planned. We would've run interference for her anyway.'

Retra's eyes widened. 'Why?'

Kero shrugged. 'We don't agree with what Eve's doing, but we don't want the Ripers to get her either.'

'But the Ripers are supposed to be our Guardians.' She wanted Kero to agree but he didn't.

'Yeah, well, it's not that simple,' said Kero. He pushed open the double doors into the club and the music slammed into them.

Kero and Krista-belle headed straight onto the dance floor. Rollo tried to entice Suki out there with him, jumping up and down in front of her, pulling faces. She laughed and glanced at Retra.

'Dance with him,' Retra reassured her. 'I'm going to look around.'

Suki gave her a wicked grin. 'Don't go beating up on any Ripers. And don't go home without us.'

Home. A strange way to think of Vank. Still, she nodded before she moved off.

Dividing her attention between the murals of sleek black birds on the wall and the faces of the dancers, Retra walked around the edge of the dance floor. The eye of each bird glittered as though lit from behind, making Retra's skin prickle.

Periodically a spotlight danced over the birds, creating a ripple effect as it passed across their wings. Retra was grateful she hadn't taken the pod earlier. The effect of the lighting and the pod together would've made the birds seem creepily alive.

At the other end of the room she discovered a dais with a small drinks station. An uther stood behind it, pouring cups of fizzy orange drink from a large brass urn. Retra grabbed the back of a vacant seat and dragged it away from the tables, to the edge of the dais. The view of the dance floor was better here and it was cooler.

She found the Leaguers were hard to pick out from the other dancers with no bandanas or bat-wing capes or spikes to identify them. Eve was clever not to have her members stand out. And Rollo had said only her close guards wore the hard leather tunics. Was it possible that Joel was one of them? Or had hope played with her imagination?

And then she saw him.

Only a few steps away from her. Moving between the dancers with quick purpose.

Joel!

She slipped off the chair and under the railing, and ran after her brother, breaking through the black lace cobweb that connected two girls, knocking into another couple.

Just as she reached him, though, the club's lights extinguished and the music stopped.

She reached out desperately, blindly in the dark. Screams rose from the club goers; delighted and scared at once.

No!

Then the glitter balls in the ceiling reignited and light dots glanced off arms and cheeks. Her hands touched her brother's shirt and she pulled him close.

'Joel,' she breathed. 'Joel, it's me.'

He stared down into her face with disbelief. 'Ret?'

His hair had grown long, straggling, and a light beard covered his jaw line. His brown eyes were the same though; alive and sharp.

'I came to find you. I couldn't bear it there any more without you,' she said.

He pulled her into a fierce hug and she could feel his heart hammering against her face. He smelt so familiar that her eyes filled with tears.

'What about Mother and Father?' he asked.

She looked up at him again. 'Mother was heartbroken when you left. So was I. But Father ... he made it ... terrible ... especially after probation.'

'They watched you?'

She shuddered in his arms. 'Yes. They sent a warden to live with us.'

Joel gripped her tighter. 'Ret, I'm so sorry. But I couldn't stay ...'

'I understand. Really I do.' Now she'd found him, the past began to evaporate.

Then an urgent voice intruded on their reunion. '*Joel! She'll be here soon ...*'

A tall, broad girl with a blunt face wrenched her brother's arm from her shoulder. The girl wore a leather vest and pants. Silver daggers hung from chains attached to her belt. Her expression was impatient. *Dark Eve*.

'We have to go,' she said.

'No!' Retra hung on.

Joel stared down into her face. Tears glinted in his eyes. 'You mustn't be seen with me, Ret. I can't explain but

you must keep away. I wish you hadn't come but there's no going back now you're here. Stay at Vank when you can – with Charlonge. Tell her I said she should take care of you. She is ... was ... a friend. Don't try to find me again. Understand? DON'T TRY AND FIND ME!'

He kissed her head then suddenly pushed her into a group of dancers. Thinking Retra had thrown herself to them, the dancers spun her from person to person. By the time she broke free and ran to the edge of the dance floor, Joel had vanished.

The aching loneliness that had been with her since the day her brother had left Grave rose up in an intolerable wave. She crouched on the floor, unable to move or speak. Her chest hurt as if she'd been stabbed.

Around her the crowd began to move, knees brushing against her shoulders, knocking her balance. She felt someone tugging her arm.

'Retra, come with us, something's happening outside!' Suki and Rollo were next to her for an instant but then they got swallowed up by the movement of bodies.

Eventually, Retra stood and drifted with the flow, not even sure what she was doing. She found herself in a short corridor that opened into a doorway as wide as a station platform. Not the front of the club, but the back.

'Retra!' shouted Suki. She stood, wedged between Rollo and a tall, thin boy with blackened teeth and a mass of gold rings in his ears. 'Here.' She lifted her elbows and shoved until the boy stepped back out of the way, leaving a gap.

The surge of people behind Retra buffeted her forward and Suki grabbed her hand, pulling her to her side.

'Lucky you came then or I wouldn't have seen you. Look!'

In front of them a glowing path curved out into the night. A short distance along the path a group of young people huddled together, encircled by another group brandishing crude weapons in their hands. The scene jolted Retra from her trance. For a moment she feared the outer group would turn and attack the unarmed ones. 'What are they doing? Are they going to hurt them?'

'It's the Cursed League. They're protecting them. Wait. Watch!' Suki quivered with excitement and tension.

The tallest of the weapon carriers wielded a blunt, heavy instrument in the shape of a cross. She was thick-set, brawny even, wearing chest armour. Glinting knives hung from the waist of her pants.

'Dark Eve has the cross!' shouted someone behind them.

'The cross from the Illi altar,' said someone else. 'She stole it.'

Another surge of spectators forced them to spill forward from the safety of the club doorway onto the beginning of the path.

Retra and Suki clung to each other and Rollo, watching as something glistening and terrible reached from the darkness to slash at Dark Eve. She swung the cross in a wide, powerful blow, bludgeoning the claws. Retra couldn't tell what it was, only that it moved with unnatural speed. Then something else attacked Dark Eve's other side, wrapping around her wrist and pulling her towards the edge of the path, towards darkness. She bent her knees and leaned back, wrestling to pull the creature into the halo of the light.

As the tussle went on, Dark Eve's strength began to prevail. The creature squealed and writhed: exposed to the light, it appeared as a mass of claws and limbs that had no real body or face.

A figure with a heavy chain sprang to Dark Eve's aid. With fierce slashes the figure beat at the creature until it let go.

'It's Clash!' shouted a voice. The crowd cheered.

Retra saw only her brother, bare-chested but with leather cuffs around his forearms. She wanted to run out to him but other things had sprouted from the dark, sinister things that sent the air putrid with stink and wracked it with a high-pitched whine. Around Retra, people cupped their hands over their ears or their noses.

'Why do they call him that? Clash?' Retra asked the thin boy behind her.

'Because of the sound his sword makes.' He pushed past her. 'I'll help you, Dark Eve!' he shouted.

The crowd cheered again and the thin boy danced about in front of them and bowed. They applauded his bravado as he sprinted off along the path.

But a few steps from the circle of League fighters something tripped him and he rolled to the edge. Instantly claws slashed his arms and stabbed into his feet until he screamed pain. The same claws dragged his spasming body into the dark.

Clash – *Joel* – ran to help him, chains windmilling. But in the precious seconds it took him to get there, the boy had gone.

The crowd fell silent, reality seeping through. Someone had been killed out there, just a little way from where they stood. One of them.

'Mother Gods have mercy,' whispered Suki. She crossed her forehead.

Rollo stared, unblinking.

Dark shapes emitting piercing cries swooped in over the heads of both the League and those they protected.

Some of the fighters detached from the outer circle and held their shields high. They thrust upward with their heavy candlesticks and swung their chains at the sky, ready to bat them away.

Suki's lips were at Retra's ear as they gripped each other. 'The draculins are hunting little bats, but if there's human blood they'll go for it too.'

Retra wanted to leave right then but her mind was numb to anything except the sight of the huddled group. What were they doing out there?

A down-gust of wind blasted them all and bright lights flooded the path. The wild draculins took fright as an enormous, bloated object, lit by downlights underneath its belly, and towed by leased draculins, descended and hovered above the League.

A gantry detached from the zeppelin's cabin, lowering on ropes until it almost reached the ground.

'Aboard,' roared Dark Eve.

The group of protected ones scrambled on to it, some slipping on the unsteady platform.

Then someone behind Retra shouted, 'Ripers!'

The crowd broke apart to make way and Retra and Suki were torn from each other's arms. A Riper brushed past

Retra, knocking her to her knees. He paused and lifted her to her feet in one effortless movement.

She stared up into an exquisite, pale face framed by straight, black silken hair.

Lenoir!

Their eyes met in the briefest moment of recognition; his, wild and hungry. She couldn't breathe, mesmerised by the intensity of his gaze.

Then more Ripers converged behind him. Modai and Test and others Retra recognised from the re-birthing ceremony.

Lenoir let her go, the withdrawal of his touch a raw energy bleed.

His eyes widened in surprise as if he too felt the loss. He started to speak to her but the call went out again, warning the League.

'Ripers!'

Lenoir turned away, summoning his band, and they ran down the path in a pack.

The echo-locaters pulled upward and the zeppelin lifted with the platform only partly retracted. The Leaguers abandoned their fight, fleeing from the Ripers along the Lesser Paths. Some of the Ripers pursued them but others stopped and began to retrace their steps.

Suki and Rollo grabbed Retra. 'Quick, let's get out of here.'

Retra felt the same panic. She didn't want to be questioned by the Ripers. 'We should go to Vank.'

But as the crowd retreated inside, siphoning down the corridor and into the larger dance area, she became parted from them again and had to catch the kar alone.

thirteen

Retra didn't wait for Suki on the Vank platform, but went looking for Charlonge straightaway. She found the Vank supervisor up in the gallery listening to the organ and staring down at the crowd in the cruciform. Charlonge was dressed in her resting lingerie, a pearly satin shift with bunches of black ribbon around the hem and neckline. With one arm she hugged a small parchment book to her chest while she held a small set of binoculars.

The book took Retra by surprise. In Grave the Council kept books locked in the library. Her mother went to the library once a week to read but the wardens had prohibited her from doing that when they put them on probation.

'Why did you lie to me?' Retra asked.

Charlonge started from her seat but, when she realised who had spoken, she fell back as if tired. 'You should be resting, baby bat.'

'I saw my brother, Joel, tonight. They call him Clash and he runs with Dark Eve.'

'Hush!' whispered Charlonge. She hastened to the end of the gallery and put the binoculars away into a small hutch, next to several other sets. Then she closed the narrow door and checked carefully to make sure the shadows were empty before she spoke. 'Do you realise what will happen if they hear this ... did y-you speak to him?'

Retra nodded slowly, absorbing the girl's nervous, almost excited, expression. 'Joel said I should stay here. That you would watch out for me. Yet you told me you didn't know him.'

Charlonge took Retra's arm and pulled her closer. 'Dark Eve is an enemy of Ixion. She breaks the rules.'

Retra pulled away in rejection of Charlonge's words. 'Rules? Ixion is supposed to be free of rules, yet it seems as strict as Grave in its own way and more ... more dangerous.'

Charlonge stared at her for a long moment. Retra saw something change in her eyes, as if a layer peeled away, letting her see further in. 'You are learning quickly, baby bat,' the older girl said. 'But then Joel's sister would.'

Retra quivered. It was not what she'd wanted to hear. She'd wanted comfort – Charlonge to tell her that she had misread the way things seemed.

A sob caught in her throat, a croaking sound like an old person gasping for breath. It took a moment before she could speak. 'Joel said that I should stay away from him. Why has he joined the League? If they find him what will happen to him?'

'He will be withdrawn.' Charlonge's lips quivered.

The chill fist of fear that held Retra's heart captive squeezed tighter. 'Tell me how you know my brother?'

Charlonge pressed her eyes with her fingers and sighed. 'We arrived on the same night – though from different places – and went through the Register together. Then we came to Vank for our first rest cycle. It stayed like that for a time: together at the clubs and the parties. I loved it here. But he was always restless and he didn't like the Ripers looking over his shoulder. He said they reminded him of Grave and his father, and that the Youth Circle was a waste of time. Then he met Eve – Dark Eve. She filled his mind with ideas.' Charlonge's face became angry. 'She took him ... from me.'

Retra bit her lip. Did Charlonge's stomach ache when she saw Joel in the way hers did when she saw Markes? 'Now he's helping Ruzalia?'

Charlonge nodded and her flush of anger drained into a look of fear. Her eyes flicked constantly to the balcony door. 'I was happy here. It was fun. Everything the pamphlets said, everything we whispered about in Lidol Push. But Joel worried about where the over-agers went. He became obsessed with it. He followed the older ones around. It became creepy –'

'My brother is not creepy,' interrupted Retra hotly.

'Others thought so ... They didn't understand his obsession with finding out what happened when you were withdrawn. Eve encouraged him. I found them ... together one night. We had a fight. He didn't come to Vank again. I don't know where he rests now.'

Unreasonably, Retra felt guilty that Joel had let Charlonge down. But Charlonge had not believed in him. Retra had always believed in Joel, and he in her. 'I want to see him again. Talk to him. Maybe I can convince him to stop.'

Charlonge's expression changed again. Hope lit her face. 'You could do that?'

'Perhaps,' said Retra. 'But I need to talk to him, alone.'

Charlonge thought for a few moments before replying. 'Then search for him again. But in the meantime you must act like everyone else. There is a likeness between you that's unmistakable; your brown hair and eyes, and the way your expressions are always so serious. After the incident with Brand, the Ripers will be watching you. If they realise that you're his sister they'll use you to capture him.'

'Modai already watches me.'

'Modai?' Charlonge was startled. 'Why do you say that?'

'I don't know. From the start, at the Register, they sensed I was here for different reasons. They tried to trick me into telling them. I'm not sure if my badge is right. They called it a faux –'

'A faux badge!' Charlonge grabbed Retra's hand and turned her wrist. The mark was beginning to glow. She stared and bit her lip. Her look scared Retra.

'What do you see?'

'I should have noticed before, when your friends brought you here. The badge is only temporary. According to Ixion law it can be revoked at any time on the word of the Guardians. You must be very careful, Retra.'

'Or?'

Charlonge dropped her hand and moved towards the gallery door. 'Or you'll be withdrawn early.' She opened the door and glided out as one practised in the art of vanishing. 'Now go and rest before you burn out.'

fourteen

Retra found the *petite nuit* rooms running off one end of the gallery. Suki was already lying in one wearing a black satin shift. Rollo was on the next bed in red silky boxers. Both had their eyes open but unfocused, telling Retra that they were deep in *petite nuit*.

She found an empty bed on the other side of the room, kicked off her shoes and slipped under the covers, not bothering to change.

Her drowse was uneasy, filled with whispers and unwanted touches, and arguments with Joel. Demons appeared then vanished to the beat of Markes's music. She searched for Markes in the dark but could only find Cal. The white-haired girl kept talking to her but Retra couldn't understand the language she spoke. Then Ripers' faces crowded in close and she came out of *petite nuit* with a start. Blinking, she looked around.

Suki was sitting cross-legged on her bed with Rollo. They were playing a finger game, trying to grab each other's first. Suki was winning easily.

Rollo noticed Retra and poked Suki. 'She's back with us.'

Suki bounced up off her bed. 'We've been waiting for you. We're starving. Let's get changed.'

Retra stretched and quickly got to her feet. Now she was refreshed, a strong sense of unease had beset her. 'I'm going to bathe.'

'Rollo said we should go to Blissed to eat.'

'Where's that?'

'Outside Bella Death,' said Rollo. 'They've got wicked sausages.'

'Wait for us while we get dressed.'

Rollo clutched his stomach. 'Wait for you? I'm surely gonna starve to death.'

Suki led the way to the *neglegere*, and talked to Retra through the screen as Retra bathed. The girl's idle words trickled over her like the water, soothing and cleansing.

When she emerged, wrapped in a towel, the room was filled with other heavy-eyed girls, peering in their lockers and chattering.

'Hey! You're the Seal who saved Krista-belle,' said one of them loudly. She was pulling on a mesh top that barely covered the tips of her breasts.

'Her name is Retra,' said Suki. 'She's going to start her own gang. You wanna join?'

Retra stared at Suki in shock.

'Whatcha gonna call it?' asked another girl with violent pink streaks through her short black hair.

'Naif's Chosen,' said Suki promptly.

Retra wanted to wrap her hand across her friend's mouth to make her stop, but Suki was fired with mischief.

'The Chosen will do what the Youth Circle is *supposed* to do. Only better. They'll make the Ripers listen.'

'Sounds boring,' said pink streaks. 'I like the League. They're way cool. Clash's gorgeous.'

'This will be more than that. Retra knows how to handle herself,' said Suki.

'We'll think about it,' said the mesh-top girl.

When they'd left, Retra rounded on Suki. 'Why did you do that?'

Suki shrugged. 'Like Krista-belle said, you're famous. In my village if luck comes your way you grab it. One time, my friend, Rani, was attacked by a bear up on the pass. It would've killed her but it slipped on the rocks and fell into a crevice. She waited for it to starve to death then she crawled down and skinned it. She came back to village with the skin on her back. Everyone thought she'd killed the bear, and she was given a place on the town senate for bravery. Her family got extra firewood and beef-chew every winter.'

Before Retra could offer comment, Suki pulled open a drawer in her locker. 'You ever worn makeup?'

Retra shook her head, caught out by the quick change of topic.

'I've been watching the others. Reckon I know what to do. Come over here.'

Retra sighed and submitted. In truth, the process of having her eyes and lips painted distracted her from worrying over Joel, or thinking of Markes, or Lenoir. She could still feel the Riper's touch, and the memory of his hungry look caused little twists of nervousness in her stomach.

When she and Suki were ready, they found Rollo.

'Hurry and get your tonics. Got mine already.' He held out his hand. A blue bead rolled around in it.

'No. They make me see strange things,' said Retra.

'Like what?'

'Demons,' she whispered.

'Demons! Don't be *fou*!' said Suki.

When she saw Retra's confusion, she explained. 'Mad, I mean, crazy like the Bonies who live halfway between our village and the men below. You know why they're called the Bonies? We used to bury our dead halfway down until we found them digging up the graves. They ground up their bones because they thought it would make them stronger. They thought they'd be able to come and take our village from us then. They are *fou* – mad from living in a place where the oxygen is too thin for them.' But then she added with a touch of grimness, 'Just to put an end to it, we burn our bodies.'

'Nice,' said Rollo.

'No,' said Retra stubbornly. 'I don't want any.'

'Suit yourself.' Suki headed into the confessional, leaving Rollo and Retra standing together alone.

Retra felt the curious glances from those on their way out to the clubs.

'You really are famous,' said Rollo. 'Everyone is looking at you.'

Retra sighed. 'Suki told some girls that I am starting my own gang. They must have told other people.'

'What?' Rollo burst out laughing. 'You?'

Retra frowned at him and changed the subject. 'Are you still going to tell the Youth Circle about the Riper you saw in Grave?'

He shook his head. 'I don't think they can be trusted. Kero thinks they spy for the Ripers. Maybe I should tell Dark Eve instead.'

'That could be dangerous.'

'This place is dangerous.'

The girls that Suki had talked to in the dressing room sauntered past them, giggling and whispering.

'Not everyone thinks so,' she said, suddenly longing to be carefree like them.

Rollo watched them as well, licking his lips in mock desire. 'I think I'm hanging with the wrong crowd. Owwww!'

Suki was back and had him by the ear, pinching it hard. 'Stop pruving, you dirty flesher.'

'Oww ... wassat mean?' asked Rollo, struggling to get his ear back.

'Pruving,' she repeated. 'Staring at girls.'

Retra hid a smile at Rollo's shocked expression.

'And fleshers are males without mates,' Suki added.

'But that's what I came here for,' said Rollo, rubbing his ear. 'To look at girls.'

'Not while you're in our company,' said Suki. 'It's rude.' She turned to Retra, her eyes already shiny from whatever substance she'd swallowed in the confessional. At least she was speaking at normal speed. 'I just heard something's happened to Markes. He was taken from one of the clubs by Ripers.'

Retra grasped her hand. 'Which club?'

'Ravens, they reckon.'

The memory of the demon images flared in Retra's memory. 'We should find out if he's all right.'

'Why bother?' asked Suki with a shrug.

'Markes helped me on the barge when Ruzalia nearly took me.'

Suki's jaw dropped. 'Ruzalia the pirate? You never told me that.' She put her hands to her hips and humphed. 'Well, that's typical. But I'm not going to Ravens again. Not after what happened out the back there.'

'Will you wait for me on the platform then?'

Suki looked at Rollo and cast her eyes upward. 'I suppose so.'

Retra smiled at her. 'Don't you mean, "I guess so"?'

fifteen

Retra walked several circuits of the main dance floor at Ravens before she saw Cal. The girl was dancing alone among the billowing funnels of smoke discharging from vents in the walls. Freshly painted tattoos decorated her arms and neck and her expression was sour.

'Cal?'

She looked at Retra without really focusing. 'What?'

'It's Retra. Seal Retra.'

Recognition slowly stole into Cal's face. 'You? Alone?' She glanced around vaguely. 'Where's your girl shadow?'

'Suki's waiting out on the platform. She doesn't want to come in here – since that boy was taken by the Night Creatures.'

Cal pulled a face. 'Thought she was the too-brave-to-care type.'

'She's brave,' said Retra in defence of her friend. 'But where she comes from they believe in omens.' Her eyes slid to the end of the dance floor and the corridor that led to the back of the club. 'Maybe she's right. Suki heard that Markes was taken from here by Ripers.'

'Who told her?'

'Some girls at the confessional in Vank.'

'So what if he was? They took him for a good reason, not bad. What's it to do with you anyway?'

'I-I ... some of the Ripers can't be trusted. I want to warn him.'

'He's with the Youth Circle and they know more about this place than you do.' Cal sneered and turned away.

Retra left the club and found Suki and Rollo standing at one end of the platform. Suki was staring out into the dark, and Rollo was staring at Suki.

'Come away from the edge,' Retra said to her friend.

'Usually it's me that's saying that sort of thing to you.' Suki's eyes were dark with eyeliner, and melancholy. 'Do you think he's dead?'

'Who? The boy ... the one that the Night Creatures ...'

Suki nodded.

Retra didn't know what to say. 'You saw what we saw. The blood and everything ...'

'Maybe they don't kill you. Maybe they just keep you out there with them.' She shivered. 'That would be worse.'

'Did you find out anything?' asked Rollo.

'I saw Cal. She said Markes was with the Youth Circle.'

Rollo gave Retra a charged look.

'We should hurry. Do you know where they meet?' asked Retra.

'Switch to the Danskoi line and get off at a station called Syn. That's all I know,' said Rollo.

Hearing the grinding of the cables, Retra pulled on Suki's arm. 'Come away. Let's go.'

They changed kars at Illi and sat together in silence as the kar climbed the mountain. Retra stared out the window. In the clear air the lights shimmered in their brilliant night rainbow formation. It should be ... could be ... beautiful if she could forget what she'd seen – what she'd heard – in the dark.

When the kar stopped, Retra got off first, followed by Suki and then Rollo. The sign hanging on chains from the stair rails read 'Syn'.

'It's Latin, you know. Means "together",' Rollo said.

'You know Latin?' asked Retra.

He shrugged, embarrassed. 'Sure. All pre-councillors know that stuff. You can't quote the law without it: *abusus non tollit usum*.'

'I know some too,' said Suki. '*Kiss my bama.*' She tapped her backside.

The pair burst out laughing and slapped hands high in the air. Retra didn't join in.

They walked down the platform's stairs and stopped in front of a wood and iron door. Rollo pushed open the door for Suki and Retra with a mock bow. Instead of a club or church, though, it led them into a plain, wood-panelled room which narrowed off into a rocky passage.

Rollo took the lead, stooping to avoid hitting his head on the overhead rock. Every few steps, the three had to press against the wall as others squeezed past them, coming out.

The cramped passage began to slant downward and Retra and Suki took off their heels so they wouldn't stumble on the uneven floor. They walked like that until Retra's back began to ache from bending and Suki had begun to curse under her breath.

The end came quite suddenly.

Around the curve of rock lay a majestic but eerie cave lit by hundreds of candles. The cooler underground air smelt of wax, and layers of volcanic red stained the walls as if seeping blood. Altars set into shallow recesses punctuated the perimeter of the cave. People sprawled on them, chatting.

'What are they doing?'

Rollo shrugged. 'Waiting for the meeting to start? How should I know? I've never been here before.' He sounded tense now that they were here.

'Where do we go?' asked Suki.

'Over here, I think.'

They walked to one end of a narrow stippled carpet bordered by red guide ropes. It ran down the centre of lines of pews; enough seating for a large audience. The carpet ended at the centre of the cave, where a rough, rectangular-shaped slab of rock larger than the cable kar platforms stood. On the rock was a table adorned with ornate, gilded handles and motifs that reminded Retra of the coffins she had seen at Grave funerals. She counted ten seated figures but only one caused her heart to leap.

Lenoir!

'Five Ripers and five of us,' whispered Suki as if reading her thoughts.

'You mean five Ripers and five of the Circle,' corrected Rollo.

'Same thing.'

'No it's not,' said Rollo. 'Circle are not us. Plenty think they're spies.'

'Who's plenty?'

Rollo glowered at her. 'The gangs.'

'Yeah. Kero the great,' said Suki sarcastically.

Retra listened to their soft bickering but it was Lenoir who captivated her gaze. He sat at the head of the table with Test at his side.

A girl with hair that fell past her knees, and a red mask painted across her eyes, appeared next to them. 'Would you like to view the Circle meeting, baby bats?'

'Sure!' Rollo gave her a wide grin.

His manner irritated Retra. How did he so easily switch to being charming?

'I'm Jaime. Follow me,' she said. 'You're lucky. They're about to begin a new discussion.' She unhooked a section of the guide rope and ushered them onto the hard wooden seats. A young man lay drowsing with his eyes open on the pew in front of them. Retra heard his deep breaths and saw the steady rise of his chest.

Jaime wrinkled her nose. 'He didn't make it to a church for *petite nuit*. This is the only other safe place to rest,' she lowered her already quiet voice, 'although Lenoir doesn't like it ...'

As if hearing his name, Lenoir stood and turned, sweeping his gaze past each candlelit corner of the cavern. His glance raked over them like the blast of a hot wind.

'Circle will now discuss the business of Ruzalia the pirate. Test?' His voice entered Retra's head, sibilant and intimate as if his lips were at her ear and his breath brushed the hairs on her neck. Her skin pimpled all over, as it had when she had first taken the Rapture pod.

Lenoir retook his seat and Test rose, the stiff frill of her hair collected into one dramatic spike that pointed out from the base of her skull. The leather of her waistcoat hugged her torso so closely that only its colour distinguished it from her skin. 'Ruzalia has attacked and boarded barges from Grave, Mustafar and Lidol Push. In each instance she has taken the older ones. We are finding less and less reaching here.'

'Then we owe her a debt, not a penalty,' said a young Circle member in a confident voice.

'Ruin. He was with Markes,' said Suki, reminding Retra.

'It is not such a simple matter, Ruin,' replied Lenoir.

With each word he spoke Retra's heart pounded in her chest and needles pricked her skin. Somehow his voice played with her senses.

'Ruzalia's raids on the barges are unsettling for the baby bats. Sometimes they become frightened and go with her on impulse. Another few were lost today. You see, she is not simply rescuing the older ones: she opposes Ixion on all counts. Guardians have been injured. She undermines our purpose.'

'W-what *is* your purpose?' asked Ruin boldly.

'Your pleasure is our purpose.' Lenoir smiled, but it did not ring true. 'Brand? You of all of us have seen the worst of Ruzalia. What think you?'

Brand. Retra's heart thumped as the scarred Riper came forward from the shadows.

The Riper's fingers went automatically to the scars on both her cheeks, tracing them along their rough ridges in an unconscious gesture. 'I say we set a trap for her and bring her in.'

'A trap?' Lenoir's voice rose in interest.

Retra's scalp-hair stiffened in response, as though his voice tugged at each root.

'Let it be known that we have a special group whose time has come. Tempt her with them. Charlonge should be one of them. She has been here too long. Flaunt them under Ruzalia's nose,' said Brand.

Suki grabbed Retra's hand. *Not Charlonge!*

'The pirate would know it is a trap,' said Lenoir.

'Perhaps. Even so, she would not be able to resist.'

'You think her that foolhardy?' Lenoir chuckled. It was a softer sound and it flowed around Retra like tepid water.

Next to her Rollo shuddered. 'What is it with him?' he muttered. 'Every time he speaks my skin crawls.'

Retra ignored him and leaned forward to the long-haired girl, Jaime. 'Where do you think they take the Peaks?'

Jaime turned her head, barely. 'The edge of the Spiral.'

'What happens at the edge?'

The girl shrugged her shoulders with impatience.

'No one knows what happens at the Spiral's edge. Some say you can fall off this world,' said Suki, with authority. 'Or burn to bits. It's been like that since the darkness came.'

'But we got here all right,' said Retra.

'The getting here's fine. Leaving is not. Or so the Ripers say,' Rollo added.

'Where does Ruzalia come from then?'

He shook his head. 'Dunno.'

Jaime raised her hand to silence them.

Rollo pulled a face at Retra, but her attention had already returned to Lenoir and the Circle.

'I think I know a way to ensnare her,' said Brand. She turned and pointed to the shadows. 'Present him!'

A Riper glided across to an altar at the opposite end of the cavern, where a figure knelt in a flowing white robe, his curling hair worn loose like a beautiful dark angel. He held a guitar carefully – lovingly – as he stood.

Markes.

He walked back to the centre altar, eyes focused on Lenoir, unaware of Retra or anyone else.

Jaime clasped her hands together. She gave a soft moan of pleasure. 'Astonishing!'

'What's astonishing?' whispered Retra.

'A baby bat being brought into the Youth Circle … that's never happened before.'

'Why have they done that?' asked Rollo.

'Hush,' said the girl. 'You'll see.'

'Who are you?' asked Lenoir.

'I'm Markes.' His voice was unnaturally thick and slow.

'Play for us, Markes,' said Brand.

Markes lifted his guitar and began the melody that had stirred so many people in Vank. For Retra it brought back the memory of how she had been after taking the Rapture pod – the abandon with which she'd danced, the desire, and then the clamouring demons. Even now the memory filled her with both chagrin and fear.

As Markes finished playing, a Riper with a high forehead and long, curling hair clapped her hands, sending the mass of bracelets on her bare arms jingling. 'Brilliant, Brand! Ruzalia has high regard for artists. Remember the singer?'

The Ripers all laughed, except Brand, who gave a sly smile. 'Thank you, Varonessa. Don't you think a boy with such exceptional talent should be honoured by admittance to the Circle?'

'Lenoir?' asked Varonessa. 'Don't you agree that it would make sense?'

Lenoir shifted his weight in the chair and crossed one leg over the other. His face, though perfectly bland, emanated displeasure. 'It's not usual to bring a new one into the Circle.'

Brand went to stand alongside Markes. 'It is not usual to find such talent, Lenoir.'

'Do you wish to be admitted to the Circle, Markes?'

Markes lifted his head and looked into the eyes of each individual around the table, returning to Lenoir last. Retra thought his eyes seemed glassy and distant. What had he taken before coming here? What had Modai given him?

'It would be my privilege, Guardian,' Markes replied.

Lenoir shrugged. 'Very well.'

'The oath, please, Brand,' said Varonessa.

The scarred Riper slid her tongue across the top of her lip and gave a throaty laugh. 'Repeat these words … I pledge to uphold the Charter of Ixion and to follow its creed to my last worldly breath.'

'I pledge –'

Dread filled Retra as Markes began to speak and she saw a demon crawl out of the cold stone floor and up Markes's body using its wet teeth as another set of hands. It climbed surely towards his neck.

No! Retra leapt from her pew and ran towards the table.

A Riper caught her before she could reach Markes, strong fingers biting the flesh of her upper arm.

She struggled to get free. 'Markes, don't!'

The demon paused and swivelled its hideous head, its many wet eyes blinking at her.

Retra choked off a scream. It couldn't be real and yet it looked so. What was happening to her? She hadn't eaten a pod like the time before.

Lenoir – all of them – turned to stare as she hung suspended in the Riper's grip.

'What is it, baby bat? Why do you seek to interrupt Circle?' Lenoir's question sounded mild, but it flooded the darkest corners of her mind like torchlight. Retra found she couldn't answer, robbed of words by embarrassment and fear. His look seared her, and in it she saw recognition. He knew her.

She dragged her eyes from Lenoir to Markes, imploring him to refuse.

He returned her look with one of surprise and confusion.

Lenoir saw their exchange and frowned. 'Aaaah … a crush on another so soon? You have excellent taste, pretty baby, but no sense of decorum, or timing. Now I will ask you again, why do you seek to prevent this boy from his service to Ixion?'

Retra grappled for words. 'I-I see danger for him – for all of you.'

'You see danger?' Lenoir gave her his complete attention now, his whole body tense with it, leaning towards her. She felt paralysed – trapped – by the weight of his presence and the glittering power in his eyes. His perfect lips fell apart, softening his face into something exquisite.

Retra's skin hurt with the comprehension of it, as if she had been burned or stung or cut. And she knew immediately that she had made a mistake, speaking of her vision. 'I mean ... we are new here and I'm frightened for him.'

Lenoir's eyebrows arched in surprise. 'Truly?'

Retra summoned all the truth she felt in her answer. All the terror she harboured. 'Yes.'

He leaned back in his chair and for a moment Retra thought he seemed unbearably sad. 'But Ixion is a place of pleasure, not fear.'

'That is not how I've found it.' Retra straightened her body and looked to Brand.

The scarred Riper moved to Retra's side with startling speed. 'May I take her, Lenoir?'

'Take, Brand?' Another mild question.

'That is ... I mean ... return her to a more suitable place.'

Lenoir gave the Riper a piercing look. 'So obliging, Brand. I hope your intentions are honourable? Unlike your previous encounter with her.'

'She seems more forthright than most. I would talk to her about unseemly displays. That is all.'

Retra heard the anger underlying Brand's soft tone.

Lenoir's eyes narrowed with mistrust, but he leaned back and draped a leg across the arm of his high-backed chair. 'Take her back to Vank. Charlonge has a talent with the awkward ones.'

'Not for much longer, Lenoir,' said Varonessa.

'Indeed, my dear. It is soon to be her time.'

Retra glimpsed his sadness again.

Brand raised her hand, signalling for assistance, and two more Ripers stepped forward, lifting Retra to their shoulders, hanging her between them like a hunting trophy as they carried her out of the chamber.

'Retra!' a voice shouted.

Suki. She wanted to call out to her friend, but her throat had closed tight with panic.

'Let go of her!' bellowed Rollo. He ran after the Ripers and barrelled against their sides, but his weight barely disturbed their momentum.

Then heavy doors closed behind her and she could no longer hear Suki or Rollo at all.

sixteen

The air grew cooler, and still. Above her, carved wood ceiling struts rose into peaks. The Ripers carried her along the corridor and finally, after many turns, into another chamber similar to the Circle room. In this one the marble-arched recesses in the rock contained stacked iron beds, not altars. Grotesques and crude crosses decorated the front edges of each arch and a mural of entwined, naked bodies ran in a fringe above them.

She shut her eyes from them but thick, smoking incense assaulted her senses.

When they laid her on a hard slab, she opened her eyes again to a dome-shaped ceiling lit by wall candles and depicting an old mural of a lamb in bloody sacrifice. Her heat beat painfully in her chest. The walls were bare rock, which seemed to press inward on her. The air was so cold she was sure she was deep inside the mountain.

Brand released her grip and began to feel her way over Retra's body.

Retra tried to wrestle free but several sets of hands held her fast.

'Brand? Should you?'

Retra couldn't see which of the Ripers questioned Brand's actions.

'Hush,' Brand hissed. 'I sensed something wrong with this one when I saw her at the re-birthing.'

'Is she a Peak?'

'No. She is young enough,' Brand replied. 'Look at the freshness of her skin, the soft pout of her lips. No ... it's something else.'

'Lenoir won't like what you're doing.'

'Lenoir does not rule. We all rule,' Brand insisted.

'But Lenoir leads,' objected the other.

Brand ignored them, reaching beneath Retra's skirt, feeling the soft flesh of her stomach and thighs.

Retra's mind flooded with panic to be touched in the way the warden had done when he came with his spying devices. Auditing, he'd called it.

Then Brand's hand stopped. The Riper keened in a dreadful, high-pitched sound of triumph. She lifted Retra's skirt above her waist.

The Ripers crowded around her naked limbs.

'Brand?'

'Brand, what ails?'

Their voices rained on Retra. She wanted to scream loudly enough to drown them out, but her Seal-disciplined vocal chords would not oblige her. Seals did not shout for help for themselves. Seals did not scream. Seals did not ...

She heard a gargle and knew it to be her own weak protest. Tears stung the corners of her eyes, more for her own choking impotence than anything else.

'I thought so,' the scarred Riper-woman gasped. She fingered the obedience strip on Retra's thigh. 'She's been hobbled.'

The Ripers stared down at it. She read shock on one face, disbelief on another, while another showed sly amusement as if party to something dirty and secretive.

Retra wanted to shrivel and die under their crass inspection of her body.

Then Brand's face came closest of all to her, blotting the others from her vision. 'That is why the Register does not trust you. You are hobbled.'

Retra wet her lips. 'No.' Her hoarse whisper echoed about the cavern.

They laughed at that, all of them; hissing noises that bounced off the walls, like excited catlings.

Brand silenced them with a turn of her head. 'This one is mine,' she said.

She drew an ivory-handled blade from inside her coat. 'Hold her still,' she hissed.

Strong, pitiless hands forced Retra's shoulders down and twisted her arms wide. More of them held her feet.

Brand climbed onto the slab and sat astride Retra, her black eyes unemotional now as she lowered the blade.

The knife's first sting on her tender skin dislodged something inside Retra's mind. She grappled to put it back in its place but it crumbled away.

'NO!' This time she shouted and thrashed, railing against them with all her strength. Desperate.

But the Ripers' weight held her fast.

No one cared for her protests, intent as they all were on the play of the knife.

It sliced into her. Two strokes, three … and then it stopped. Brand's fingers probed the wound she'd made and tugged.

The obedience strip tore from her thigh in a spray of warm liquid.

Brand held the bloody sight aloft and gave a hoarse crow.

Faintness crept upon Retra. It called her towards a numb, white oblivion. But a voice snatched her from its release.

'Brand! What barbaric thing is this?'

The Ripers melted away, leaving the scarred woman alone astride her.

'Look, Lenoir. I am freeing her. She was monitored. Hobbled.'

'You've cut her to do that? Hurt her. What about Enlightenment, Brand? Would that not have been a better way?'

'Why would she deserve that?' Brand traced bloody fingers along her face scars, leaving clotted trails.

'Why wouldn't she? She's an innocent.'

Brand thrust the grisly strip at Lenoir. 'Innocence is but another constraint. Ixion is not a place for innocence.'

'Fool. You have torn her artery! Wounds like this need deep sleep to heal and she can no longer do this. *Petite nuit* is not enough. You risk her premature death. Ixion is not a place for that. You will be disciplined for your actions!' The voice that projected so easily across distance now filled the chamber like a pouring of foundry lead, crushing whatever it fell upon.

Lenoir struck Brand with a gloved blow that sent the Guardian crashing to the floor.

His gaze fell to Retra and the searing heat of it seemed to cleanse her. 'Graselle, take the girl and prepare her,' he said.

Retra sensed another person at her side but her eyes remained with Lenoir. Beautiful, so beautiful ... to see him this close almost took away her pain.

Or maybe the woman carrying the burning candle, who'd crept close to her at Lenoir's bidding and put her hand hard on the wound, had done that ...

seventeen

'Retra, listen to me. I am Graselle. If you want to live you must be Enlightened.'

Retra heard the woman but couldn't see her. She lay in the dark of a curtained recess and smelt the cavern's incense around her still. Soft moans nearby. And, more distant than that, chanting.

Her heart moved in slow, lethargic beats. 'Where – am – I?'

'This is a secluded crib kept for those who ail, or are dying in a way that is not prescribed.'

'Am I dying?'

'If you're lucky you will be,' whispered a fever-pitched voice on her other side.

Retra turned her head on the pillow to see who spoke but the darkness was too thick for her barely open eyes.

'Shut your loser's mouth, Lottie. You did not heed our rules so you paid,' said Graselle.

'Beast-woman,' whispered back Lottie. 'Nothing more. Lenoir's pet.' She started to cough.

'You ignored the rest rule and now your body has failed. You were greedy. You had your time and you burnt it too quickly.'

Neither said any more.

Slowly, Retra began to distinguish outlines. Graselle, she discovered, sat at the end of her bed in a high-backed chair, her pale face as grey as the moon behind clouds.

The sick girl, Lottie, lay across from her in another bed, her knees drawn up.

'I feel strange,' Retra said softly. 'Heavy. And something is cutting my leg.'

'It's a tourniquet. Your body can't stop the bleeding. It's struggling to heal the wound because you can no longer sleep,' said Graselle. 'It drags all your energy for healing but it is not enough. Your mind must help it.'

Retra let Graselle's words float and settle in her mind. 'How do I do that?'

Graselle stood and began to rub her arm with a cool, scented lotion. 'Your kind shouldn't come here. The change is too great for Seals. Yet you have chosen it and rejected your society, so you must learn quickly or perish.'

Lottie thrashed her legs around. She moaned again, loudly this time. Damaged sounds. 'Give me ... something ... it hurts, Graselle. Please ...'

'It is against our rules.'

'Please help her,' Retra begged. 'She sounds –'

'No! It's forbidden.'

'What if you were her?' Retra begged. 'What if you hurt like her?'

She sensed Graselle hesitate.

'I'll see what I can do.' She disappeared between the curtains.

'Thanks,' Lottie panted. The unpleasant taint of her sweat drifted between them.

'What happened to you? What's wrong?' asked Retra.

'I burned too bright. I saw too much.' She cried a little then.

Retra wanted to comfort her but as she tried to sit up blood trickled from her thigh wound and she lay down again, afraid. 'What did you see?'

'I saw what happens to us ... I know where we go ...'

'You mean when we're withdrawn? You know what it means?'

But Lottie rambled on then with words that made little sense: half-finished thoughts about her sisters and her home.

Eventually she fell to a kind of murmuring quiet that lulled Retra's senses. Perhaps the girl was not as sick as Graselle had said. Perhaps she had just taken too much of the tonics and would recover.

But, suddenly, Lottie came upright. She stumbled across to Retra, grasping her with hot, shaky hands. She climbed onto the bed and fell across Retra's chest. Her breath began to rasp. 'Mama ... I want Mama ...' Tremors wracked the girl.

Retra obeyed an instinct that ran deeper than her Seal training – deeper than anything she knew. She patted the girl's back, soothing the distraught stranger.

After a while the tremors eased and Lottie sighed, nuzzling into Retra's neck.

Then she became heavy and still.

Forever still.

Graselle came back too quickly and Retra knew she'd been waiting outside the curtains, listening.

'I – can't – breathe,' Retra gasped.

Graselle pulled Lottie's body roughly from Retra, levering it onto the other bed. 'Knew it wouldn't be long before she went. They get angry for a while before the end, and then they want their mama. They always want her.'

Retra couldn't stop her tears. They poured down her face and slid around the nape of her neck.

Mother.

Graselle lit a small candle on the wall behind Lottie's bed. 'They'll come and get her soon, while she's still warm,' she said almost to herself. 'But we must prepare you. I'll cover her or you may find her a distraction.'

She drew a cover from a large chest of drawers at the foot of the bed and laid it across the dead girl.

It did nothing to calm Retra. Her teeth chattered and the silent tears turned to sobs.

'Shut up!' Graselle slapped her once, across the cheek. 'You don't have much time yourself.'

Retra didn't care. Not even the thought of Joel mattered right now. Even in Grave, Mama came when you called. Mama cared when you were dying.

Retra wanted to go home.

Graselle shook her arm. 'Stop it! Lenoir will skin me if you die. He's got a point to prove with Brand.'

When Retra didn't stop, Graselle slapped again and again until the stinging and the force of it broke through her misery and replaced it with anger. The tears dried up and the Seal in her returned.

'That's better.' Graselle stripped the last of her clothes and sponged her thigh with warm water. With each wipe, the sponge filled with blood. She muttered her disapproval in short harsh syllables as she re-packed the wound hard with clean white cloth. 'Should – stem it – enough – give him – time.'

'Time?' Retra whispered. 'What for?' She felt drowsy, slowed by the efficient movements of Graselle's hands, and the life seeping from her.

Graselle leaned her face in close. 'Drink this!'

She lifted Retra's head so she could pour cool drink into her mouth, dabbing the spills with her fingers. It tasted like honey and lemon.

Then she put the cup down and lifted Retra's shoulders from the bed, sliding a black silk shift over her head and arms. 'It'll be hard for one like you but don't fight it. Give in to it and all will be well. He'll heal you.'

She laid Retra back down then and attended her feet and hands, rubbing them and then dabbing the toenails with something that Retra couldn't see.

Lastly, she rubbed scent in the bend of her elbows and behind her ears. Then she dressed her hair as if she were pampering a favourite doll.

Panting with her efforts, she straightened and arranged the silk across Retra's breasts. 'There. You're not beautiful, but something, sure enough,' she said to herself.

eighteen

Ripers carried her through more tunnels, so many different ones that she lost sense of time and direction. She'd become separated from her surroundings by a mind-mist, but a vague, innate sense told her that they climbed upwards.

When they stopped, she was dimly aware that the Ripers' shoulders heaved with effort. They collected themselves for several moments before they entered yet another cave, this one kept private by a door.

Incense had played along the rocky passages but now it choked Retra like thick smoke. A Riper coughed with it.

'Lay her on the bed and wait outside.'

She knew his voice and immediately she felt better.

When his hand touched her, she forgot Ixion, forgot ... everything.

'You don't have much time – you are bleeding to death slowly. The cut that Brand inflicted upon you will not heal because you cannot sleep. There is only one way your body can recover. I will help you increase the endorphin levels in your body.'

If she could have, she would have asked what that meant. But she had no way to make her tongue work.

When he kissed her, it took time for the pressure to register on her lips. Even then the sensation was dull and without thrill.

'Come back to me, little bat,' he whispered.

She wanted to, but his face drifted above her, neither solid nor real. Dimly, she felt the bed move, lifting her body higher in a gentle, floating movement. Not a normal bed but a cloud, she thought.

His tongue found her face, and with delicate strokes he licked her skin like a catling cleaning its hairless baby. His tongue was warm and rough and the trail of wetness tingled and bought her senses to life again. He blew gently down and her skin pimpled with the cool stickiness.

She felt his hand at her thigh, sliding up across the silk. She heard him groan. Disappointment? Revulsion? Or something else? What did the deep sounds in his throat mean?

Retra didn't know.

She knew only that he licked her wrist now, moving upward to her shoulder, each trail returning sensation to her numb skin, bringing warmth and tingling promise. His hair spilled over her in a shining spread.

Then suddenly his face was up near hers and their breaths mingled.

'You must know what I do for you and understand that afterwards you will be mine.'

His eyes were neither warm nor loving. But there was something in them. Purpose, she felt ... and possession. His hands swept the pillows around her into a pile, forcing her shoulders higher than her hips.

'Watch!'

Retra watched.

He lowered his body until his face was level with her thigh. With a quick movement he lifted her skirt and peeled away the white cloth that covered her wound. Fresh blood spurted and with another quick movement he fixed his mouth to it.

Retra cried in pain and disgust. Her mind rejected his action and yet, as his lips pressed against the wound and his tongue probed its depth, the pain lessened and a soothing sensation spread through her body.

As he worked, not taking from her, but pressuring with his tongue and mouth, life returned, energy pouring inward. Soon enough, her thoughts became clearer. She writhed, trying to slide away from him, but he levered his body over hers and trapped her with his weight.

The pain she had lived with for so long now diminished to a faint throb and she became light with its absence.

In its place, other feelings began to grow. A strange pressure in her abdomen that made her want to shift again but in a different way. She reached for Lenoir's hair and grasped a handful, tugging it without concern for him, her breaths quick. The pressure inside her turned to a sensation she had never felt before, never thought could exist. It propelled and exposed her, and she rocked and shivered against him.

The sensation peaked, forcing her body into a high arch.

Her mind unfastened. Her body sparkled.

Then it was over and she collapsed.

As the intensity waned and his hair had slipped from her grasp, Lenoir raised his head, the evidence of her wound emblazoned on his lips.

'You are now mine.' He raised his body until their faces were level again. 'So tell me, baby bat ... what is your name?'

She thought about it for a while. There had been another name, but she no longer belonged to it.

'Naif,' she said, finally.

part two

naif

nineteen

Lenoir had her taken to a room close to his own. Naif learned that from overheard whispers between Ripers who watched outside her door, and from Graselle, who came to tend her.

'He's put you near him,' Graselle muttered, as she sponged Naif down. 'I'm not sure why, but it's different. He wants something from you and he'll get it. Which means you'll have power.'

Even though she was recovering, Naif felt reluctant to talk. Her mind still struggled to absorb what had happened.

Instead she examined the whitewashed room. It appeared, like the other caves, to be carved from the rock of Ixion. The walls were impregnated with crosses and statues like the Grotto and the heavy wood and iron bed she lay upon was made up with white linen sheets.

Graselle emptied the basin of washing water into a bucket and pulled the clean sheet up past her waist.

Naif closed her eyes. She didn't wish to think of her body at all, or Lenoir, but Graselle's words had fashioned a filigree of hope around her sickened heart. *Power.*

'Look at me,' demanded Graselle.

Naif's eyes flicked open. Graselle was so close that she could smell her perfumed skin and see the moth-shaped flecks of black in her tawny eyes.

'You know what Enlightenment means now?'

Naif glanced away but Graselle would not have it. She seized Naif's chin with strong fingers and forced her to look back at her. 'Tell me what it is.'

'It's ... I think ... it's ... *pleasure*,' Naif gasped.

'Pleasure. That's right. And that's what you came here for. To Ixion.'

'No – I ... I ...' But Naif could not say the rest. She'd lost the trace of her purpose.

'Everyone comes here for pleasure. Even if they think they don't. Embracing it is harder for some and they go mad before they truly accept it. Most of the places they come from are founded on guilt and rules. The Ripers want us to break away from that – some wish to tear it from us while others are more subtle.'

Guilt and rules. Grave was like that. But it seemed so far away now. So distant. Grave belonged to Retra, the person she was – not Naif.

Graselle went on. 'Lenoir fights his own battles. There's plenty here among the Guardians that would be him. He has to show Brand that he's still the one with the power. Perhaps by turning one like you – a Seal – to pleasure, gets him more kudos ... or per'aps ...'

'Wha-at?' croaked Naif.

'Per'aps he just fancies you.'

Naif forced more words out, something to distract from the notion of Lenoir finding her attractive. 'He says ... I owe him ... my life.'

Graselle collected her washers and the bucket and went to the door. 'And you do. But the "owing" works both ways. He'll have got what he needed from you. But there's a bond between you and Lenoir now and others will know it. Watch yourself.'

'How do you know all this?'

A sheen of moisture glazed Graselle's eyes. 'He has bonded before.'

'To you?'

'You don't speak of your bonding to anyone. See,' Graselle hissed.

After Graselle left Naif lay, thinking, feeling. Something had changed inside her since Lenoir had healed her. Her body was no longer shadowed by pain. But more than that, her mind felt so light and free that it might fly away.

'Naif?' Lenoir was standing at the door, watching her. The intensity of his gaze thrilled her. She had expected to be repulsed by him, but strangely she felt only fascination and gratitude.

'Yes?'

'In the Circle chamber you said you saw danger for the boy, Markes.'

Naif slid her feet to the floor and sat up on the edge of the bed, feeling only a little dizzy. 'It was ... nothing,' she said. 'You spoke of sending him out to attract Ruzalia. I was frightened, that's all.'

'Why do you care what happened to him?'

His question confused her. 'What do you mean? Why does anyone care for ... anything? I-I like him, I suppose, and I w-wouldn't want him to be hurt.' It was the truth. Markes had protected her from Ruzalia, and been kind to her when Cal had been so cold.

'Ixion is a place for hedonism. Selfishness. Yet you've risked dire consequences to help others. What makes you do that, I wonder?'

Naif tightened her arms around herself in defence. 'I am no different than anyone else.'

He thought about what she said. 'Perhaps not. But Enlightenment has saved your life and freed you from your moral restraints. You will feel different. What I am curious about is whether the selfless part of you died with its release. Is it the rules and restrictions in your life that have made you self-sacrificing? Is guilt the foundation of kindness?'

He came over to the bed and sat down, placing his hand gently on her injured thigh in an intimate gesture. 'I will watch and see. You are well enough to move around Ixion as before. There is only one difference. We are bonded and you will come to me when I require it.'

'Why would you?' Naif asked.

Lenoir's smile was enigmatic. 'That I could not predict but I may need you at some time. Now tell me, little Naif, what do you know of Dark Eve and Clash?'

Naif's heart thumped at the sound of her brother's chosen title. Did Lenoir know her secret? Was he probing her honesty with their bond? 'I will not spy for you,' she said quickly.

Lenoir's expression became curious. 'It is merely a question.'

She strived to keep her face composed. It seemed harder now that she was no longer that other person – the Seal, Retra. 'I saw them outside that club where the boy was taken by the Night Creatures. They're passionate in their beliefs,' she said.

He surprised her then by sighing. 'They are misled – as passion most often is. Beware it, baby bat. Beware the foolishness of passion.'

'The League believes that those of us who are too old to remain here are taken away by you and ...'

'And what, Naif?'

She spoke quietly to soften the accusation. 'They believe you kill us.'

Lenoir curled his lip in deprecation. 'If that is the case, and we are such villains, why would I have saved you? What is your life worth if we are murderers?'

'I am wondering about that, Lenoir,' whispered Naif, addressing him directly for the first time. She had a sudden urge to keep him talking so that she could learn more about Ixion. 'Was it to prove yourself in some way to the other Guardians? A show of your strength against Brand?'

'There is that,' he admitted freely, without annoyance. 'But not that alone. Can you guess the other reason?'

She shook her head, not sure that even her newly freed self was ready to hear his reason. 'You said at the meeting that Charlonge was to be withdrawn soon.'

'It is true, her time is close. Does that concern you?'

'She has helped me, as she has helped so many others. And she'll be frightened.'

Lenoir did not reply.

'Why do you need to keep mystery around it? Have you thought to explain what *does* happen to the Peaks? It's the unknown – the uncertainty – that scares people. Understanding might help matters with the League as well.'

'So wise and yet so naive, little bat. Doesn't uncertainty also create ... excitement?' His voice stroked her, like gentle fingers on sensitive skin. 'Don't you burn brightly because of it?'

Naif knew he skirted the topic, distracting her. 'But keeping secrets has a cost.'

'I would put your mind at rest and say that Peaks transcend to the next phase,' said Lenoir.

'The next phase?'

'Of pleasure. Ixion exists as an antidote to the rules and conventions of other places. We believe that indulging in pleasure will make better people. Self-denial and discipline and virtue are all myths invented to control you.'

Naif considered the idea. It was true, her Seal training had been a shackle, but it had also been a comfort. She was unsure, still, about the new person inside her. Would she like who she now was? She shrugged. 'I guess so.'

'You must trust me that aging and withdrawal will bring you to something better.'

'Then you should tell this to the League.'

'Not all the younglings are as easy to convince or as rational as you, little Naif. Your lack of ego makes you receptive. Some thrive on combat, or the promise of it. Some on notions of heroism. Others prefer not to know anything at all. Not everyone seeks the truth.'

Was Joel like that, Naif wondered? Did he thrive on combat? She'd never thought him as a natural agitator and yet ...

'I seek only to protect them but the League bring trouble on themselves by assisting Ruzalia. The pirate is a hazard to our lifestyle, our system.'

'P-protect them? From who?'

'Brand is not as tolerant as I am.'

'Is that why Brand attacked Krista-belle? To provoke you?'

His eyes narrowed, and Naif saw his mood change. He got up and walked to the door. '*I am the dominant Guardian.*'

'But surely Brand challenges you with her actions.'

'Yes. But she will be disappointed.'

twenty

Graselle returned with fresh clothes. Naif noticed her eyes were red-rimmed from crying.

'Graselle?'

But Graselle refused to speak and, after helping Naif to dress, she went away without a word.

Soon after, the two Ripers guarding her door entered. They led Naif through the labyrinth of tunnels to the surface, leaving her on the Syn platform.

Though it was only hours since she'd been here with Rollo and Suki, it felt as if days had passed. Would they notice the change in her?

She caught the kar to the closest club, eager to find them, but her faux badge began to glow at Club Abraxas. By the time she reached Bella Death it became hot and uncomfortable and fear of exhaustion forced her to seek rest close by at Goa.

The church of Goa reeked of decadence. From the jumble of makeshift altars decorated with gaudy fringed silks, painted figurines and ugly dolls, to the thousands of mirrors and murals of naked feasting. Perhaps Rollo's story of the warring provinces on Ixion was true. Goa couldn't have been made by the same people who built Vank. Goa was a place for worship but not holiness.

She took her *petite nuit* in an untidy room next to the apse which was overflowing with bodies. As soon as she'd rested, she left and sought the servery. The serving platters were spread haphazardly around and the white linen cloths on the tables were stained with food spills. There was none of Vank's order or hygiene or supervision. She looked for uthers but couldn't see them. Perhaps they didn't come here.

Eating as quickly as she could, she went to wash and change her clothes. As she entered Goa's *neglegere*, a girl approached her.

'Are you the Seal who's forming the Chosen?'

'No. My name is Naif and I'm not a Seal.'

'Shame.' The girl seemed disappointed. 'Everyone's looking for her.'

'Who is everyone?'

'A red-headed guy and a Stra'ha'ine girl. So are the Wings, and the Freeks and the League. Apparently the Ripers have taken her and it's causing a big drama. They're talking about rescuing her.'

Naif's stomach clenched. She must find Rollo and Suki before they did something foolish.

She left Goa immediately and went to Vank. Though Rollo and Suki were nowhere to be seen, Charlonge was standing by an uther near the hot server, presiding over meal time.

As Naif entered and walked between the heavy, polished tables, a quiet descended upon the normal murmur and clatter.

'Where have you been?' Charlonge gripped her elbow when she got close enough. 'Come with me.'

Naif let Charlonge steer her up to the gallery.

The older girl shut the door behind them and locked it. Then she went to stand over by the balcony balustrade. She seemed nervous. 'Everyone's been talking about you. Is it true you were taken by the Ripers? What happened?' Charlonge wrung her hands so anxiously that it made Naif want to take them and hold them still.

'Char, you're going to be withdrawn soon.'

Charlonge was silent for a moment. 'How could you know such a thing?' She sounded angry, not scared.

'Lenoir told me.' Naif hoped that the darkness of the gallery hid the rush of heat that warmed her face.

'Since when do you have conversations with the dominant Guardian?'

'Brand tried to – *did* – hurt me. Lenoir has healing powers and I was bleeding –'

'Bleeding?'

Without the shame she would have felt as Retra, Naif lifted her skirt to show the healing wound on her thigh.

'Lidol saints, what is that?' gasped Charlonge.

'When Joel ran away from Grave, the wardens sewed an obedience strip on my thigh, to stop me leaving the compound. I had to learn to manage pain to escape. Brand tried to ... she took me ... and found it then she cut it out.' It was hard to say even with her newfound confidence.

'Cut it out!' exclaimed Charlonge. 'Did they dull the skin?'

Naif shook her head. She smoothed the skirt down. The memory was too sharp to linger upon. 'I am healing. While I was at the Youth Circle meeting, before Brand took me, the Ripers spoke of you. They said your time was over and that they would use you and Markes as bait to catch Ruzalia.'

'Markes? The guitarist?'

'Yes. You must decide what to do before they come for you.'

'Decide what?' Charlonge left the balustrade and paced a couple of steps.

'Whether to trust Joel and escape. Or let the Ripers use you. Lenoir says that withdrawal means we go to a better place.'

Charlonge turned to her. 'And who do you believe?'

'I don't know. Truly. You should talk to Joel.'

'What did Lenoir say exactly?'

'Lenoir says that withdrawal is the next part of our evolution into pleasure but –'

Charlonge trembled. 'I need to think. And you must go and find your friends. Stop them before they do anything reckless. They were planning to come after you.' She went to the door and unlocked it.

'Do you know where they are?'

'A party has been called at Agios. Everyone is talking about it but only some have been invited.'

'Invited?'

Charlonge gave a sad smile. 'Yes. Check your locker in the *neglegere*.'

Naif went to the *neglegere* as Charlonge suggested. She found a single garment hanging in her locker: a black brocade dress, stiff and beautiful and encrusted with hundreds of shiny gems. As she took it out, a pair of tiny lace gloves fell free from it, and a gold-trimmed card.

'Wow! Oh, put it on,' said a girl standing at a locker close to her. The girl looked a little like Suki, but taller, with honey-coloured hair and full lips. She wore a cherry red mini with high-legged boots and a velvet-fringed tank top.

Naif slipped off the simple silk shift she'd chosen at Goa, not as bothered by modesty as before. The brocade was difficult to get on and she had to wiggle and tug and ask the girl to lace the back. Finally she got it into place. The bodice fitted tight and low over her breasts but fell away into a froth of lace that trailed onto the stone floor.

'You look like a bride,' said the girl. Then she giggled. 'Well, sort of ...'

Naif's heart skipped a beat at that. *Whose bride?*

'You must be going to the party at Agios. It's gonna be amazing. That new musician is playing there, the tall, gorgeous one that everyone loves. I think his name is Markes.'

Naif picked up the invitation. 'A-are you going?' she asked.

The girl pouted. 'It's formal wear only and I don't have an invitation or anything like that in my locker.'

Naif held out the card. 'Do you want to take mine? And the dress.'

The girl's jaw dropped. 'You'd give me *that*?'

Naif shrugged. 'I could wear the silk.' She pointed to the shift from Goa on the floor. 'But I warn you, this dress isn't very comfortable.'

'Aren't you the one who smashed the scarred Riper with a chair?'

After a moment, Naif nodded. It would be impossible to get away from what she'd done. Perhaps she shouldn't try. 'But I've taken a new name. I'm Naif now. I'm not a Seal any more.'

'Most people take on a new name when they come here. I like Naif. It's cool. I'm Geen. And thanks for the offer, but it wouldn't fit me. You're smaller than I am.' She headed to the door of the *neglegere*, her boots making clicking sounds on the stone. 'Have fun at the party. Maybe I'll see you around.'

twenty-one

Naif took a cable kar up the mountain to Agios. At each stop excited partygoers climbed in; boys in formal suits, some with white jackets and tails, and girls wearing long dresses, crimson velvets and clinging silks.

Naif bundled up the lace train of her dress and rested it on the seat next to her, to discourage company. She stared out of the window at the twilight and tried to identify the different shimmers; Vank and Illi below, Agios and Los Fien above, light spatters that marked the clubs, and the light trails of the paths winding together and then branching off into the faint strips of the Lesser Paths.

It's like a blood system of veins and arteries, Naif thought, and the sight of fainter trails made her quiver. What type of creatures lived in the true dark of Ixion?

Though seeing Joel fight had terrified her, her fear was tempered with pride at the knowledge of his valour. He had fought the Night Creatures and bested them, at least in that moment. Who knows how many still existed out there in the dark?

For the first time since coming to Ixion, Naif pondered on how Ixion really worked. Why did the Ripers appear so ageless? Where did the uthers get their raw material – food and cloth? What were the uthers to the Ripers? Servants?

The kar's arrival into Agios station interrupted her musings as the laughing partygoers piled out onto the platform, racing each other down the stairs. At the same time another kar swung in from the opposite direction and she heard stampeding of feet on the overhead bridge.

She got out and looked for Suki or Rollo among them, but most wore masks with their formal clothes. The crowd channelled down towards the wrought-iron gates of the church, where Ripers stood at the door checking dress standard and invitations.

The noise and crush of bodies gave her a moment of panic but she let it rise and then subside. Markes would be inside somewhere, she hoped.

'What are *you* doing here, Seal?'

It was Cal, wearing a soft white halter-necked dress the exact colour of her hair. A string of black beads fastened across her forehead in a delicate headband gave stark contrast. Her heels must have been high because she looked down on Naif.

'Hello, Cal. I'm no longer a Seal. My name is Naif.'

The press of bodies forced them closer together as it bottle-necked at the door.

'You've come chasing Markes again, I s'pose – like all the others, now that he's one of the Youth Circle. Well, he's not interested in you, you know,' Cal sneered. 'We're already exclusive.' She gave a sly look. 'As much as you can be here anyway.'

For the first time since they'd met, Cal's antagonism didn't intimidate Naif. 'Why are you so threatened by me?'

'Pardon?' Cal's eyes widened in surprise as they were pushed forward again.

'Invitation!' demanded a Riper in a full-length leather dress and mask. She held out a hand encased in a chain-mail glove.

Naif recognised her as one of Lenoir's followers. She handed over the gold-trimmed card.

The Riper glanced at it.

'My apologies, Naif. I didn't recognise you in the dress. Please step this way.' The Riper indicated inside the church to a door between two columns.

'But, I'm with Markes – the musician,' said Cal, waving her invitation before the Riper. 'I should get in before her.'

The Riper ignored Cal and gave a small bow to Naif. 'Lenoir wishes to see you.'

'Lenoir?' Cal gasped. 'Then the rumours are true. I didn't believe them.'

'Naif?' Test appeared alongside the first Riper. She gave a short bow and also gestured towards the columns. Both Ripers seemed nervous of keeping Lenoir waiting.

Naif didn't want to see him but nor did she want to create a fuss. She glanced at Cal. 'Maybe I'll see you inside. You can finish telling me about Markes.'

The girl's open mouth was the only answer she got.

Naif followed Test through the door and up a set of stairs that led to a gallery similar to the one in Vank – though much wider and grander. Her feet sank into a soft floor covering, so unexpected after the wood and stone of most other buildings.

Lenoir leaned against a wooden railing, exquisitely carved in the manner of a laden grapevine. He held a fluted glass in his hand and stared down into the cruciform with a pensive expression that made Naif's heart thump.

While she waited at the door to the gallery, Test approached him and spoke quietly in his ear. Lenoir jerked from his reverie and glanced at her. Though his expression remained unchanged, Naif felt a honeyed warmth emanate from him and spread through her body. For some inexplicable reason her presence pleased him.

'Come closer, batling,' he said. 'I'm pleased that the dress is ... as it is. Please join me.'

He held out his hand for her and watched intently as she walked towards him.

Unsteady legs carried her across the balcony. She had not expected to see him again so soon. And not like this.

Lenoir, however, seemed in no hurry to speak. When he did, finally, his voice was a mere whisper. 'I had thought you might enjoy the view from here before you join your party.'

Naif peered down into the cruciform. Agios was a church like no other she had seen. No austere furnishings and heavy wooden beams, or alcoves darkened by crosses. Neither was it gaudy or cheapened by crude figurines.

Agios glowed with candlelit, gold-inlaid marble that enhanced the sumptuous satin friezes of hunting scenes and feasts hanging from its walls. It reminded Naif of her mythology lessons about the incredible Marble City of Marsoucee.

'What do you mean by ... my party?' she asked.

'When we bonded, I learned much about your desires. You craved fun but did not know how to have it.'

She stared at him, not knowing what to say.

'I have something for you.' With deft fingers he slipped a jewel bracelet around her wrist – blood stones, dark red and cool to touch.

'Beautiful,' she breathed.

'Like you, baby bat.'

Something caught in Naif's throat. Lenoir's compliment – like his gift – was unexpected and untruthful. She did not compare to the rich, cool beauty of the bracelet – nor did she want to. 'I don't think so, really.' She cast a quizzical look at him. 'And nor do you.'

He laughed at that. 'No. You taste much better than ancient gemstones. And I for one should know.'

Naif removed the bracelet and returned it to him. 'I owe you my life, Lenoir. We have a bond. But please don't ... give me things.'

His face grew stony. 'Do you seek to order me around like Brand?'

'Brand?' Naif caught her breath in anger. 'How could you tar me with her brush?'

He sighed, his flash of annoyance leaving him as quickly as it came. The troubled look returned to his eyes. 'Brand wishes to lead a hunt against Ruzalia. She has called an extraordinary meeting of the Guardians. We will vote on it in two passes.'

'Is that usual? For you to vote on things, I mean.'

His expression became so intense and angry, lips thin with it, that she wondered if he might lose control. 'We have never voted before. Not while I have led.'

'How long has that been?'

He took her lace-gloved fingers in his own and turned it over to touch the bare circle of her palm. He traced his fingers across the skin as if drawing a picture. 'Since we came.'

Naif frowned but left her hand in his, hoping he would say more. 'I don't understand that really. How did you come to be here?'

Even though she said the words casually, without demand, he dropped her hand at once. 'For one who has had little conversation in her life, you make it too easy to talk, Naif. I must remember that.'

Immediately, she missed the warmth of his hand on hers, the contact of his skin.

'Enjoy the party. It's for you. Learn about pleasure.' He averted his face in a clear dismissal.

Test appeared next to her as if she had been standing there all along.

'This way, baby bat.'

'Please don't call me that,' she said as she followed Test down the stairs.

The Riper stopped short of the last step. She cocked her head to one side, her mouth twisting in a cold smirk. 'Of course. If you say so.'

Naif wondered if Test really supported Lenoir. Something about her manner seemed disdainful, like Brand.

The Riper stepped down onto the floor and waited for Naif to pass her. 'Make sure you keep to the well-lit paths,' she said.

It seemed more a threat than a warning.

Naif hurried away from her and into the grand hall of Agios proper.

Inside, the partygoers had assembled in nervous groups, spilling out from the transepts into the nave. They sipped from long-stemmed glasses and the girls tottered on the highest of heels. The boys tugged laughingly at their bow ties and tightly buttoned satin vests. At the far end, a long table covered in white linens divided the narthex from the rest. As Naif gravitated closer to it, she saw how laden it was with all manner of food: silver trays piled with cheese, fruits, rolled meats and honey-drenched pastries. If she concentrated hard she glimpsed uthers scurrying to and fro.

Her mouth watered, but as she reached for a tray the first strains of music filled the room and thought of food left her. The ambient candlelight was extinguished and the high altar fell into the spotlight. Markes sat there, cradling his guitar.

Naif pressed her stomach to ease the sudden constriction. Even from the narthex she could see his hair down curling past his shoulders, and the dreamy expression on his face.

The simple chords he picked with his strong fingers pinched at her skin. Dancers slowly filled the nave, some with partners, some alone, wrapped in their own private worlds.

Naif was drawn out with them, the soulful pull of the music impossible to resist. She let her body move with it, revelling in her newfound freedom to dance.

Gradually, the music built pace from something slow and sensual to a loud and prolonged strumming frenzy. Then the music peaked and finished softly.

As the dance area slowly cleared, arms bear-hugged her, lifting her from her feet and shaking her. 'Retra?'

'Rollo!' Another set of hands broke the grip of the bear hug and insisted she be put down. 'Suki!'

'Are you all right?' they cried, in unison.

Suddenly she was surrounded by people: Krista-belle, Kero and the Wings. Beyond them she could see others – spiked wristbands peeking out from under their suit sleeves – trying to get closer. The Freeks were all there as well.

Their welcome radiated an alarming energy and she took a deep breath to inhale the charge she got from it. 'I've been looking for you all. Charlonge said you might be here.'

Kero pointed at Rollo. 'He says that Brand took you.'

While most of the faces around her looked relieved and happy, Kero's face was serious.

Naif nodded. 'She did. I just talked to a girl at Goa who told me that you were coming to find me?'

Kero shrugged but Krista-belle hugged her. 'Yeah. That Brand's totally got it coming.'

Naif returned the hug then gently pushed Krista-belle away. 'Brand's dangerous. Don't go anywhere alone.'

'You weren't alone, and it didn't help you,' pointed out Suki.

Kero came closer. 'What happened? How did you get away?'

'Lenoir helped me.'

Everyone began to talk at once, asking questions about Lenoir and Brand.

Kero cut across them with a low warning. 'Scatter!'

The group obeyed, spreading to different sides of the dance floor as Ripers entered the nave and headed towards them. Naif could see Test among them. She glanced to the balcony. Was Lenoir watching as well?

Seeing the group dispersing, the Ripers altered their course and sauntered over to the food tables as though that was their original intention.

Markes started another song and Suki grabbed Naif and leaned in close.

'What happened to you? Rollo's been *fou*, swallowing everything in sight since you were taken by Brand. He thought they'd killed you and he blamed himself. He got the Wings and the rest of them all worked up. They're all ready to fight the Ripers. Been stealing torches from the churches so they can see better in the dark. I got a knife – just in case.' She pulled a blade made from sharpened cutlery from the pocket of her waistcoat. 'I told him I could look after myself, and so could you. He said you couldn't – that you were a Seal.' Suki rolled her heavily shadowed eyes. 'I said you could be a stink-worm but you could still look after yourself. Guys! Just 'cos a girl's a bit quiet they think she's feeble.'

Naif couldn't help smiling. 'There's no need for knives.'

'So where did the Ripers take you?'

'I'm not sure, exactly. Somewhere inside the mountain. Brand tried to do something horrible to me, but Lenoir ... stopped her. I lost blood and I ...' Naif clasped her hands together, not wanting to tell Suki the rest right then with Lenoir so close. 'Lenoir healed me. After *petite nuit*, I was able to leave. I went to Goa and Vank looking for you before Charlonge told me about the party.'

Suki hugged her. 'You don't have to tell me. I know it's hard for you to share things.'

But Naif took Suki by the shoulders and looked her straight in the eyes. 'I *do* want to tell you. Something did happen. I'm not a Seal anymore, Suki. My new name is Naif.'

It took a moment for the meaning of her words to sink in. Suki frowned at first then she grinned. 'You've taken an Ixion name? Hooray!' She did a little dance.

'And I *will* tell you everything that happened, in time,' said Naif, determinedly. 'The important thing now is that I talk to Markes. Lenoir told me some things.'

'Lenoir?' Suki gave a near-hysterical laugh. 'You're as *fou* as Rollo! Nobody talks to Ripers.' Her gaze flicked over Naif's shoulder and her expression became sombre. 'Speaking of ... Modai's watching us from behind that column. Let's dance,' she said.

Modai. The sound of his name made every muscle in Naif's body tense but she forced herself to entwine arms with Suki's and they moved out onto the dance floor, closer to Rollo. She tried to loosen into the music like before, but Modai was there, at the edge of her vision, every time she moved and turned.

Rollo sidled closer and his arms found her again. She didn't try to shrug him off. Even his sweatiness seemed preferable to the Riper's scrutiny.

'I freaked out,' he said in her ear. 'Why did you do that? Why did you try to stop Markes from joining the Circle?' He squeezed her tighter.

'You heard them. They're going to use him as bait for Ruzalia.'

'But what you did ... right there in the meeting ... and you think *I'm* reckless. I got scared when Brand took you. I tried to stop them.'

She shifted in his embrace so that her head rested against his shoulder. 'I know, Rollo. Thanks.'

'What happened when they took you, Retra?'

'Naif.' She looked at him the same way she'd looked at Suki. 'Call me Naif. I don't want to be a Seal anymore.' Not after Lenoir. Not after Lottie.

He nodded. 'Okay. Naif. But what happened?'

She lifted her head a little just so her mouth reached his ear, but not so she could see Modai. 'Brand took me somewhere. She hurt me but Lenoir stopped her. Afterwards he talked to me. The Ripers are divided over more than Ruzalia, Rollo. If Lenoir loses his following among them, I think we're all in danger.'

He leaned his cheek against hers and she felt his body quiver. 'You *talked* to him?'

'Yes.'

'You believe the things he said?'

'I'm not sure. I think I do. In a way.'

They moved together to the music for a while before Rollo spoke again. 'I went a bit crazy after they took you. When the Circle didn't lift a finger to help I knew that I couldn't tell them about the Ripers being in Grave. They may not all be spies, but they're weak. They mean nothing and do nothing.' Even through the noise of the music he sounded disappointed. 'There's something else but you mustn't tell anyone else. Not even, Suki. She'll just laugh.'

'What?'

'I've joined with Dark Eve.'

'No!' Naif stood still, making him bump into her and stand on her foot. Her ankle gave and she would have fallen if he hadn't grabbed her waist.

She righted herself, wincing. Then she thumped her fist into his chest and glared at him. In the amber candlelight his skin looked sallow and his eyes glittered with brittle excitement.

'*Foul* Why did you do that?'

He disguised his hurt with a belligerent look. 'Because they want to change things here like I wanted to do at home. Only I was too scared of the Council. I told Eve about the Riper I saw in Grave, and about the Ripers' plan to catch Ruzalia. She told me that my information was really important, and that she wanted me to join them. She's amazing, you know.'

Amazing. That's what Joel had called her. 'Join her to do what? Carry her weapons?'

He opened his mouth to answer and then snapped it shut. He shook his head at her as if he would say no more.

Naif's anger swelled easily and unchecked. 'You've already told me you've joined them. It's a bit late to start keeping secrets now.'

'Well, maybe I shouldn't have told you anything.' He hunched his shoulders. 'I was just … relieved you were all right. Fross knows why, now? You're so weird. Here you are putting me down for wanting to change things here, and yet look at the things you've done. Smashing a Riper with a stool and then trying to stop the Circle inducting Markes. At least the Leaguers are welcoming and they tell you what they're going to do next. You're so random.'

'You think because they're *welcoming* it makes the things they do right? That's just stupid.' The angry words continued to tumble from Naif's tongue.

This time hurt showed plainly on Rollo's face. 'Why are you always putting me down?'

Her wave of anger turned quickly to guilt. Was he right? Was she treating him the same way that Cal had treated her? Yet he frustrated her.

'And anyway,' he said, 'I think it's *stupid* pretending you can talk to a Riper. They tell you what to do and you listen. That's all.'

In truth, though, Naif didn't know what she really thought about the Ripers. She was – would always be – loyal to her brother, but Lenoir had saved her life. And he seemed so genuine about wanting to protect them all against Brand.

Rollo let her go and she stepped away from him. The gap between them quickly filled with dancers, and a moment later she could no longer see him or Suki.

Or Modai.

Confused and disconsolate, Naif let the music draw her to the front of the nave where she could watch Markes.

His gaze lingered on her for a moment as he shifted from something fast into a ballad with a mesmerising melody. Couples stopped dancing and reached for each other.

Naif stood perfectly still, so as not to ruin her harmony with the music. This song was for her – she knew it – and she let it sweep her from her unhappiness to a place of pleasure. It was like being with Lenoir again, having his warm tongue against her thigh, his breath on her skin. The memory of her Enlightenment seemed as fresh as if it had just, this moment, happened.

When the music finally stopped she felt raw with emotion. She hovered at the jube that separated the dancers from the nave, waiting for Markes to climb down from the altar. But others had the same idea and she had to cling to the screen to keep a position at the front.

'He wrote that song for me,' the girl next to her told another. 'We met at Illi.'

Naif flushed with embarrassment, realising her foolishness. *All* the girls thought he'd written that song for them. She read it in their faraway looks, on their parted lips. His music did that – made everyone feel special.

The girl suddenly stumbled into her. 'Fross, sorry!' she said. 'Someone pushed me.'

A figure with moon-white hair, wearing a halter dress, elbowed her way past them both to climb over the jube and saunter right up to the altar.

'Who does she think she is?' said the girl angrily.

Cal.

Markes slid down and began packing his guitar into a case. He glanced up at Cal as if startled by something she said. Then his gaze roamed the crowd until somehow it found Naif again. He closed the lid of the case and walked straight over to her.

The girls screamed for his attention but he didn't seem to hear them. He stopped in front of Naif, leaning down to her.

'I've been looking for you. What happened?'

Naif glanced around nervously. 'Not here.'

He frowned and nodded. 'Come.' He put out his hands and lifted her up over the jube. Others tried to follow them but Ripers appeared and pushed them back.

'What are you doing with her?' said Cal from behind them.

'I want to talk to Retra. Hold my guitar and wait here,' he replied, as he drew Naif past the altar into the darkened depths of the sanctuary.

'They brought me in through a side door. Let's go out through there.' He dropped a casual arm over her shoulder, which sent her heart spinning. She hadn't been this physically close to him since the barge. Could Lenoir see them? She glanced back into the light of the nave and transept. She couldn't make out the gallery from here.

'There,' said Markes. He pointed towards a deep, shadowy apse that contained a tall, iron stand. Upon it rested an unlit candle, as large and broad as Markes's shoulders.

As they got closer to it, Markes dropped his face to hers and nuzzled into her neck. For an instant her world filled with the same melody he'd been playing. Her head swirled and her heart soared.

'What –'

He lifted his head and peered through the curls of his fringe into the light at their backs. 'In case someone is watching us,' he said. 'Looks like we're doing … what everyone else here is.'

Naif wanted to reach up and pull his face back to hers, but burning fingers of anger reached across Agios and gripped her throat. *Lenoir!* She gasped and edged away from Markes.

But he didn't seem to notice anything, intent now on leading her behind the statue to the outline of a door, where he fumbled with the bolt for a moment before it came free.

Naif stepped through first.

He followed her out in the warm night, standing under a small pond of lantern light. From where they stood, paths led across and down the mountainside, each marked by a faint glow.

Now that they were truly alone, Markes let go of her and pulled his sweat-damp shirt loose from his waistband. He slipped his hands into the pockets of his pants. Shoulders hunched over a little, he kicked the toe of his boot into the dirt.

'Why did you try to stop me from joining the Circle? You act so weird around me. Like at Vank.'

She couldn't tell him about the demons. Even Suki hadn't understood. 'That time in Vank, Modai made me eat an entire Rapture pod. I didn't know what I was doing.'

He lifted his head, startled. 'Why did he do that?'

Naif shrugged. 'I don't know but he seems to follow me, and watch me.' She shuddered. 'At the Youth Circle, I had a premonition. You know, like something bad might happen to you.'

'But it's an honour to become a member of the Circle. Cal says you're just jealous.' He frowned. 'But I don't think you're like that. Are you?'

'The Ripers want to use you and Charlonge as bait to catch Ruzalia.'

'What?'

'We heard them speaking of it just before they brought you to the circle.'

'I don't remember much, other than meeting Lenoir. Bran gave me something to swallow. Said I needed to take it if I was to be presented.' He frowned as if trying to recall what had happened. 'I don't trust them or the Circle. You've heard of the gangs here?'

'You mean the Wings and the Freeks and whatever?'

She nodded. 'Plenty of them think that the Circle spy for the Ripers.'

Markes raked his fringe away from his eyes, and for the first time she saw them properly. They looked cloudy as if he'd taken something; a pod or beads.

'I don't know what to believe. Did you know that some people are talking about you like you're some sort of hero?' he said. 'And others say *you're* the one that's been spying for the Ripers. That Lenoir's watching over you especially.'

'Who says that? Members of the Circle?'

Markes dropped his head again.

'Lenoir helped me when I was hurt – that's all.'

'You got hurt?' Markes glanced at her and his expression became halfway apologetic. 'I didn't know. Was it Brand?'

She nodded.

'Look, you're kinda strange, Retra – but nice. Must be the Seal thing.' He held out his hand. 'Thanks for being worried about me, but do me a favour and just let it go.'

She would have been grateful to him – when she was Retra – for the handshake and the kind words. But Naif didn't care so much for his stubborn ignorance. She kept her hand at her side. 'My name is Naif now.'

'You've taken an Ixion name. That's cool. I'd better get back then, *Naif*,' he said.

'To Cal?'

Markes rolled his eyes and grinned. 'She's nicer than you think. Underneath, I mean. It's just her way to be ... direct. Her father is a warden.'

Naif felt sick. A warden as a father. What would that be like? The warden assigned to watch her family had been so cruel. 'There something I've wanted to ask you. In the compound we weren't allowed to play music, or listen to it, unless Father approved. Was it different for you?'

'I come from a family of church musicians. We're allowed to be trained for that purpose.'

'So musicians beget musicians. Wardens beget wardens, and councillors beget councillors,' said Naif. 'I didn't know that was the rule. My father was a prayer leader. I ... girls could not be prayer leaders.'

He nodded. 'Seals are different.'

'So Cal would have become a warden if she'd stayed?'

He nodded and looked uncomfortable. 'Look, are you coming back inside?'

'Soon.'

'Don't take too long or the Ripers'll come looking for you. People are saying this party is for you. Is that right?'

She shook her head. 'Why would there be a party for me? I'm just the same as everyone else.'

Markes gave a half grin. 'Yeah? I don't think so.'

He left her then.

twenty-two

Naif crouched down and hugged her knees, feeling curiously deflated. What had she been hoping for in their conversation?

She wasn't sure. Her emotions kept changing. Smiling came more easily, but so did dissatisfaction. All the checks and measures she'd learned as a child had crumbled away, leaving turmoil.

'Ret?'

The whisper drifted up from one of the paths that led down the side of the mountain. She peered along it. She knew the voice but couldn't see him. 'Joel?'

'Walk towards my voice but don't look down.'

Her heart quickened and she did just as he said, feet crunching the light gravelly surface. Dry brush broke off and caught in the train of her skirt. She bunched it up and kept walking.

'Stop now and fold your arms. Just stand looking down the mountain at the lights. Keep your voice low. Ripers might be watching.'

'There are no Ripers out here,' said Naif.

'They are everywhere, little sister.'

Naif badly wanted to look at him. His voice came from a fall of rocks close by. He must be crouched behind there.

'I heard you'd been taken by the Ripers. What did Lenoir do to you?' he demanded in an angry whisper.

'N-nothing. It was Brand. Lenoir saved my life, Joel.'

'Tell me,' he demanded.

Naif took a breath to explain again. 'The wardens gave me an obedience strip when they put us on probation to stop me trying to leave the compound.'

'What did it do?'

'It gave electric shocks if I went near the gate to the compound.'

'So how did you get away then?'

'I practised hurting myself to get used to it, so I could escape.'

'You *practised* hurting yourself?'

Naif licked dry lips. 'The way you told me. It was all I could think of to do. I couldn't stay there after you left. Mother was heartbroken. She barely spoke. And the warden, he used to ...' She stopped there, unwilling to share what happened, even with Joel.

'Ret, I'm sorry.'

She gave a tight little nod. 'Brand found the strip and cut it from me. I was bleeding, dying, when Lenoir ... he stopped the bleeding.'

'Brand used a knife on you?'

'She's cruel and dangerous, Joel.'

'And she will pay for this,' he said with whispered fury. 'How did she know you?'

'She tried to tear my clothes off at the re-birth, and then I interfered when she attacked one of the White Wings – a girl called Krista-belle.'

'With the chair? I heard it was you but I didn't believe it.'

'What Brand was doing ... was like the warden and I-I got angry. Anyway ... Brand and Modai have been watching me.' She took a breath. 'Suki and I and Rollo went to the Youth Circle meeting. They are going to use Markes as bait to lure Ruzalia. I tried to warn him against joining them but Brand took me from there ... and she found my obedience strip. When she cut it out, it tore my artery. Lenoir came and stopped the bleeding.'

'Lenoir?'

'Yes. Lenoir is trying to protect us all. He says the Peaks go to a better place; he calls it the next stage of pleasure.'

'You believe him?'

Naif took a deep breath. 'I-I do. I think. At least, I believe he believes it. But the Ripers are divided. Brand wants to take over from Lenoir. They're voting on it in two passes. If Brand wins, they'll hunt the League down. All the gangs will be disbanded.'

Joel made an angry sound. 'Your friend, Rollo, came to us with a similar story but we weren't sure if he was telling the truth. I must warn Eve. We'll make sure Ruzalia knows. Is there anything else you can tell me?'

Naif's heart gave a painful thump. Suddenly she felt used. 'I'm not your spy, Joel. I'm your sister. I don't want to be a part of any gang. I want you to come with me. To leave Ixion.'

'Leave?' said Joel. 'Why would I want to do that?'

Naif clasped her fingers together. 'This place – it's not how it's supposed to be. It's –'

'Flawed? Dangerous?' said her brother. 'Just like Grave. But I can change Ixion. Eve has shown me that. In Grave I couldn't do anything. The Council, our parents, they suffocated us. But Eve has plans here. She's amazing. I wish you knew her.'

'Can you really change anything, Joel?' Naif couldn't keep the bitterness from her voice. She'd longed so much for her brother's company again, gone through so much to reach him, and now … 'Do you just want to be a hero?'

Joel didn't like her questions. 'What's happened to you, Ret? You used to believe in everything I did. You made it bearable for me at home, and I tried to protect you. Remember when Father found the *Angel Arias*?'

'Of course I do,' said Naif fiercely. 'And do you know how it felt when you left? You didn't even tell me you were going.'

'I couldn't,' he protested. 'It was safer for you that way.'

'*Safer!* Did you even *think* about how it would be afterwards? Father punished me every day for what you did, and Mother cried. She just cried all the time.' Naif felt her anger returning. She wanted to shout at her brother.

She'd never been angry with him like this before. Seals didn't behave like that. But she wasn't a Seal anymore. Lenoir had changed that. Lottie had changed everything. 'Then the wardens came and put their electro-eyes in my bedroom. They watched me when I bathed and … Joel, they watched me do *everything*. And if I tried to leave the compound … *the pain*.' She touched her wounded thigh automatically.

His silence might have been guilt. Or indifference. Naif had no way of knowing without seeing his face. And she longed to do that. 'Joel? Please ...'

'I'm sorry,' he whispered. 'Bye, Ret.'

'My name is Naif,' she replied.

Nothing. No rustle of the bushes, or scraping of gravel. But she knew he'd gone.

'Joel, wait!' She started down the path after him. 'Please come back.'

But when she stopped again to listen, all she heard was the faint strains of music from Agios and a scrabbling sound.

She swivelled, catching the slash of a dark figure in her corner sight. Not Joel. He wouldn't try to scare her like that.

Where was Agios? She could no longer see the church. Her haste had taken her past a large rock face that jutted above her now, obscuring the view behind.

Just follow the path back, she told herself.

But the path – so well lit before – had dimmed with barely enough light to see one step ahead. Naif began to retrace the way she thought she'd come, but the bare dirt disappeared and her feet became tangled in undergrowth.

She stared blindly into the dark, seeing only the outlines of low bushes and, further down the mountain, the brilliant webbed lines of the kars.

Away from the pungent musky scent of the church, the dark smelt dangerous and charged with energy, as if lightning had just struck the spot where she stood.

But there were no storms on Ixion, just the constant, prickling heat.

Naif heard scrabbling again, a few feet ahead. And to the left. Then behind. Something circled her, or more than one thing. Dread twisted in her stomach. Modai had warned her. Test had warned her. *Don't stray from the path.*

She wanted to run but didn't know which direction to go.

A snuffle and then a soft squealing; a long tail lashed out from the bushes. It tore through the delicate material of her dress and little barbs hooked into her ankle.

She collapsed and the tail began to drag her, the barbs sawing into her ankle bone. She couldn't fight it, couldn't think above the depth and height of her pain.

She moaned and writhed in its grasp but the pain only intensified. Spines scraped her face, wrapping around her arms as it dragged her deeper into bushes.

Then, as suddenly as it had attacked, the creature let go of her ankle. The release from pain brought an ecstasy of relief, but the elation vanished as it threw its entire weight upon her legs and began sucking at her bleeding ankle.

She tried to move but it shifted in counterbalance, sniffing and nibbling, working its way up her body until it sat on her chest. It touched her hair, playing with the strands and tugging them.

See you. Follow you. Want you.

Naif forced her eyes open to confront it; a smooth-skinned creature from what she could see, with a small, almost human-shaped torso. But ungainly, clawed limbs sprouted from its lower body, and tentacles curled out of its shoulders. Or were they unformed wings?

And its face ... so appalling. So utterly bestial.

Pity eroded some of her fear. Instinctively she reached out and touched its face.

The creature grew still, startled by her action.

She traced the contour of its ridged forehead with a trembling finger. It felt slick, coated in a layer of mucous, and the flesh underneath sprang back like bed foam.

The creature tilted its head forward, making it easier for her to reach.

Naif scratched gently along the ridge and it made little grunts of pleasure.

They stayed together, in that position, until her arm began to ache and the weight on her chest became impossible to bear. 'I must ... sit up,' she whispered.

The creature cocked its head as if thinking. Then it shifted its body, easing the pressure on her lungs.

She lay, gasping in air, for a few moments. But as she tried to sit up, its body became rigid. In one quick movement it leapt to its claws, gripping her flesh for balance. The sudden weight crushed the breath from her lungs again and her head began to spin.

She tried to roll and catch her breath, but it was too agile, and merely adjusted its stance. She grappled for its ankles to push it away but her hands slipped on her own blood.

'Naif!'

She heard her name like a roar in her head; a piercing cry of anguish. And then the beast was gone, knocked from her by an attack from another powerful being.

'No!' Naif struggled to sit up as the two forces battled close to her. 'Lenoir! Stop!'

The creature screeched – at first in anger, and then in pain. Their bodies thumped and tumbled and Naif's mind filled with the terrible crack of breaking bones.

The path began to glow again. She could see it just a body length away. She'd been close to it all along, only a few steps.

Gritting her teeth she crawled towards it, ignoring the prickle of spine bushes and sharp twigs, until she felt the smooth packed gravel underneath her body. Her fingers clutched the hard pebbles and tears of relief spilled down her face. She crawled along it towards the edge of a rock face. Around the edifice would be Agios. If she called out, if she –

But as she reached the rock, Lenoir appeared before her, his silken hair hanging in strings, wet with blood, and his cloak torn away.

'Are you hurt?' He loomed over her.

She tried to sit up. 'I didn't think ... it would ... harm me. It wanted to be ... petted.' Her tongue had trouble forming the words, too dry to moisten them properly.

Lenoir dropped to his knees and pulled her into his arms. 'It would have killed you, Naif.'

Naif swallowed and tried licking her lips. 'Wh-why do you say that?'

He stared out into the darkness. 'Leyste has been following you since the moment you left the Register.'

'Leyste? You've said that name before. Who is Leyste?'

'Leyste is a Night Creature who likes to linger around the new ones. This is the first time, though, he has stalked one.'

Stalked. 'Yes. He spoke to me outside the Register. And other times. But I was the only one who could hear him.'

'The Night Creatures have our ability to place sound. It is not usual that they use words, though.'

Naif thought about how Lenoir's voice seemed so close to her when he was speaking to a crowd. 'H-how m-many c-creatures are out th-there?'

Lenoir lifted her as if her weight counted for nothing and began to carry her back along the path. 'There are many and their form varies.'

He didn't look at her or speak again after that.

As they climbed closer to Agios, Naif's adrenaline faded and pain replaced it. Her ankle began to throb and the cuts and scrapes on her skin stung. She clamped her lips together so as not to moan.

The music grew louder – not Markes playing, but a fast, discordant sound – and Lenoir's arms involuntarily tightened around her. 'What were you doing out here, Naif?'

She tried to think before she answered. Despite her anger at Joel, she would never betray her brother to anyone. But Lenoir was clever and she was not practised at lies.

'I came outside to talk to Markes – the musician. We … argued and I walked away. I lost sight of Agios when I passed the rocks. Then the path faded.'

'Leyste,' he said the name grimly, almost as though he was angry with himself. 'He found a way to tamper with the light relays. I had not thought him clever enough. Nor any of them. Not unless …'

Naif lifted her head from his chest. They'd reached the side door that she and Markes had used, but Lenoir walked straight past it, along the high stone wall, towards the rear of the church.

'Neither of us can go inside Agios looking like this. I'll take you to Vank. Charlonge will clean your wounds.'

'You think that Graselle has probably seen enough of me?' Naif gave a soft, humourless laugh.

'It is not safe in the Dominion while the vote –' He cut off his sentence as they turned around the corner of the church.

A dull, metallic, octagonal compartment half the size of a cable kar and lit by its own spotlights sat alone on a flat piece of ground. Test leaned against it, frowning. When she saw Lenoir she straightened and opened a door in the side of the compartment.

She stood back then, arms folded, legs astride, her whole stance disapproving.

Lenoir didn't acknowledge Test at all. Instead he lifted Naif inside onto a softly upholstered seat and climbed in after her.

A rush of memories hit her: the brass trimmings of the interior, the deep scent of the leather seats. It could have been one of the Grave Elders' horse-drawn carriages. She'd travelled in them with Father to probation hearings, his anger like a priest's grille between them, her shirt damp still from her mother's tears.

A sudden jerking movement forced her to grasp hold of the seat.

'The carriage is merely unfolding its legs. In a moment you'll feel nothing,' said Lenoir.

Naif held on until the rocking sensation stopped.

After a couple of reassuring glances out of the window, she settled against the seat and let her eyes close. She drifted to a place where neither thought nor action dwelt; an in-between place of nothing – away from the pain.

'Naif!' Lenoir roused her from *petite nuit* with a rough hand. 'Take this now or the pain will harm you.' He pressed a pod into her hand.

Remembering what Graselle had said to her about healing, she didn't argue. She chewed it carefully and waited for the effects.

It wasn't long before heaviness crept into her limbs, dulling everything including her reticence. Her head felt woozy but in a more pleasant way.

She glanced over at Lenoir. He stared moodily out of the window, his lips pursed. His beautiful hair matted by dark blood.

She wanted to ask him about Leyste but other words came out of her mouth. 'Why was the party for me? You said that before when we were in the gallery,' she asked.

Lenoir didn't look at her. 'If the vote goes against me things will change. I will not be able to do the things I choose. I wanted you to see how beautiful parties can be, how elegant.'

Naif gave a spontaneous smile. 'That got messed up, didn't it?'

He shrugged dismissively. 'We are here.'

Naif sat up straighter, wondering if the pod had distorted her senses. 'We've only been moving for a few minutes.'

He turned to her now, his face almost unsightly, streaked with blood and wearing an oddly vulnerable expression. It frightened her to see him that way.

He reached a hand to her face and the fingers that had burned her skin in Agios felt warm and soothing. He kneaded her cheek between his thumb and forefinger.

'I thought that Leyste had already killed you, baby bat.'

'I s-still don't think he'd have hurt –'

He pinched her skin and let go. 'Yes. He would.'

There was something so convincing in his tone that she let the argument go.

He leaned towards her until his mouth found the graze above her lips. Then he licked it gently, as he had done once before, like a catling with its baby.

Naif's body dissolved, all sensations nullified, other than the pressure of his tongue and the tingling wetness of it. Obeying a welling of instinct, she shifted under his touch until her lips aligned with his. She pressed up hard against him. Her lips opened artlessly and her tongue found its way to his. He tasted salty with the tang of her blood, but that flavour ebbed and another took its place. She craved the moisture, thirsty for more of his special taste.

His fingers clamped around her upper arms, lifting her from the seat onto his lap. With every gentle pull she made on his tongue, he clung tighter to her, as if he would compress her into a tiny portion of herself.

Sensation, numbed by the pod, returned to her body with such crashing intensity that it left every nerve raw. She wanted to scream with elation and with pain.

Lenoir's teeth closed on her tongue and raked the sides of it, causing her to arch in his grasp.

A growl ripped from his chest. He pushed her away and she glimpsed his face, so contorted that she barely recognised him. His cheeks seemed to have grown fuller, concealing his bone structure, and his brow heavier. His lips curled back, revealing the glistening of his gums.

'Lenoir,' she gasped.

He flung her back onto her seat and fled from the carriage.

She didn't try to follow him. It seemed as much as she could do to lie across the seat and gather her fragmented mind. What had she just seen? Had his face really distorted? Had the creature Leyste been as dangerous as Lenoir insisted? Why wouldn't Joel listen to her? Her thoughts chased each other in circles.

'Retra?' Charlonge peered anxiously through the door. 'What are you doing in Lenoir's carriage? What's happened? He came storming into the church and told me to come and tend to you. I've never seen him ... upset.'

Naif struggled to concentrate on the rush of questions – she had so many of her own, and her ankle throbbed in time to the beat of blood at her temples.

'It's Naif,' she whispered. 'And I think my leg is hurt.'

'Naif? Isn't that the name I picked out for you?'

'Yes.'

Charlonge nodded approvingly then stared down at her torn clothes. Her eyes widened. 'You mean legs, arms, stomach ... Let's get you inside. You can tell me what happened later. Has Lenoir given you anything for the pain?'

'Pod,' croaked Naif.

'A whole one?'

She nodded.

'Well, that explains why you're so dreamy.'

No, thought Naif. *Not just that.*

Charlonge helped her into Vank. The carriage had stopped adjacent to the lower platform, making it only a few steps to the door and away from the clutching dark.

Naif thought she saw the carriage jerk upward on long spidery legs and disappear. But she couldn't be sure, because everything had become strangely blurred.

Even Charlonge ...

When *petite nuit* dropped away and her mind cleared again, she found herself in Charlonge's bed again, covered in red silk sheets. Charlonge sat at her black escritoire reading a large book. Naif knew it to be old from the crackle of the stiff pages and the musty smell that rose from it every time a page turned.

'Where do the books come from?' She asked it softly so as not to startle the older girl.

Charlonge put the book down. She seemed relieved to hear Naif speaking normally. 'Each church has a library.'

'What are you reading?' Naif felt a sudden yearning to touch it. The library in Seal South had been her place of solace, and frustration. But she'd only been allowed to read about religiosity and etiquette and comportment.

'Ixion history,' said Charlonge in an offhand way. 'Newbies always want to know things and sometimes I can't answer them.'

'What sort of things?'

'Mainly about Ixion itself and how the Ripers came here. But sometimes they ask about the Tri-suns and cosmology.'

'Cosmology?' Naif had never heard the word before.

Charlonge sighed. 'I suppose you've never even heard of the Tri-suns?'

Naif shook her head.

'It's not your fault, Naif. These things have been kept from you on Grave. But you should know, at least, that we live on a world that spins around a cooling star.'

'Abraxas. Yes. Joel told me.'

'Did you know it also has two companions?'

'There are three stars?'

'Imagine three friends arguing and sending one into exile. That's our suns.' Charlonge closed the book. 'And before you ask me any more questions let me see your wounds.'

Naif sat up against the pillows and pulled the silk shift up to her thighs to inspect her legs. Other than the circle of heavy bruising around her ankle, all of the scratches had almost healed. Her arms were the same. She slid the shift down quickly, not knowing what to say.

'I've heard that Lenoir is a healer,' said Charlonge. 'But how is that possible? On your face as well.'

Shame and a little excitement burned inside her. As before, Lenoir's tongue had healed her. 'I'm not sure ... but one of the Night Creatures attacked me when I wandered from the path near Agios. Lenoir found me and fought it. Killed it.' She forced herself to say the words – to make it real. 'Then he brought me here. That's all I really remember.'

'That's all!' Charlonge picked up a cup and walked the length of the narrow room. 'Take this.'

Gratefully, Naif sipped the proffered grape juice.

Charlonge waited until she had finished. 'What were you doing out there?'

'I-I went with Markes, so we could speak privately.'

'The musician?'

Naif nodded and drew her legs up to her chin. 'We talked for a while and then he went inside. I would have followed but Joel called out to me.'

'Joel?' Charlonge's fingers fluttered. 'What did he say?'

'I tried to get him to understand that Lenoir wants to protect us. Joel doesn't believe me – we argued and he left, and I lost my way a little. Leyste was waiting for me. Lenoir said he had been stalking me since I came through the Register.'

'Leyste?'

'A Night Creature.' Naif hugged her legs to her chest to hide a shudder. 'He was hideous, Char, but sad in a way.' She sighed. 'Lenoir said he would have killed me.'

Charlonge took several careful steps away from the bed as if to avoid breaking something underfoot. 'Lenoir is showing you great concern, Naif. It's not usual for a Guardian to do that. Are you sure he's not trying to reach Joel – through you?'

Naif shrugged. 'I don't think he knows.'

Charlonge stared at her. 'Don't be sure of anything with Lenoir. The Guardians aren't like us. You can't predict what they'll do. You can't *know* them, Naif.'

Charlonge's words triggered a thought. Naif slid off the bed and had to steady herself against a wave of dizziness. 'The vote!'

'What're you talking about? You need to rest. I don't want Lenoir punishing me for –'

Naif seized Charlonge's hands. 'The Guardians are voting on what to do about Ruzalia. If Lenoir loses the vote then Brand will be their new leader. She'll use Markes as bait for Ruzalia. And you as well. She'll hunt down the League and the gangs. Do you know Brand, Char?'

Charlonge swallowed nervously and nodded. 'Of course. The scarred one?'

'I have to go to the meeting and hear the result.' Naif let go of Charlonge's hands and straightened. A powerful wave of determination flooded through her. 'If Brand wins then I must warn everyone.'

Charlonge stood still. Naif saw warring desires in her changing expression. And fear.

'Have you decided what you will do, Char?' she said softly.

'Yes,' she said, finally. 'I'm coming with you.'

twenty-three

The Youth Circle meeting chamber stood empty apart from the girl with the long hair and the mask painted across her eyes, who drifted, distracted, around the table, tugging at the heavy chairs, fingering the polished stone.

'Jaime!' called Naif, stepping onto the narrow strip of carpet. Charlonge stayed behind her.

The girl jumped and stared. 'You!'

'I'm Naif. Where are they holding the Guardians' vote?'

'How do you know about that?' The girl came closer to her, the soft folds of her skirt making faint, sliding noises as it caught between her legs and brushed against itself. 'Only the bonded know about ...' Then her eyes widened. 'You're the one they're all talking about. The one Lenoir protects.'

Naif hesitated. Though she didn't like Jaime's insinuation, it was the truth, somehow. 'Where is the vote?'

Jaime pouted and she crossed her arms. 'He used to have time for me before you came along. Now he doesn't even touch my hair. They say he's obsessed with you.' She looked Naif up and down. 'I can't see why.'

Naif's face flushed at both the insult and the thought of Lenoir's attentions.

She automatically reached for her Seal training to calm her but it wasn't there. She must trust her instincts now, and they told her to be forceful. 'Tell me where the vote is or I'll set the Night Creatures on you.'

'Naif!' exclaimed Charlonge from the shadows.

Naïf ignored her. She didn't have time to debate with either girl.

'*You* can't control the Night Creatures. Only the Guardians can do that.' Jaime flicked her long hair behind her shoulders with assurance, but Naif heard the tiny waver of uncertainty in her voice.

'They'll come and find you, I promise,' Naif whispered. She pulled the hem of her skirt up and showed her wounded ankle. 'They almost took my foot off before I learned their secrets. Now I can speak to them – command them, if I wish. Imagine what they would do to your hair out there in the dark among the thorn bushes and the dirt.'

The girl took a step backwards. She pointed to an apse-like alcove lit by a single wall-mounted candle on the far side of the cavern. 'That way. But I don't know where. I never go in there.'

Naif ran across the cavern, hoping that Charlonge followed. She must find out if Lenoir survived.

The door in the alcove led into a cave that was lit by torches hung from the walls. But tunnels branched off it in so many directions that she stopped abruptly.

Charlonge bumped into her shoulder. 'Do you know where to go? If you don't know we could get lost.'

'Shhh!' said Naif. 'Listen!' The faint strains of guitar melody reached them, echoing around the cave. 'Markes. But which way?'

'The Dominion is a series of concentric circles connected by short corridors,' Charlonge replied.

Naif stared at her. 'How do you know that?'

'It's in the books. Before the Ripers lived here, the caves belonged to the monks. They drew pictures of it. It's like a maze.'

'Is that what you've been studying?'

'I knew my time was soon. I wanted to know more before I ... left.'

Naif felt relieved that Charlonge had been acting – thinking – for herself. 'I'm glad you did,' she said. 'Circles mean that we can't get lost.'

An unbidden confidence surged through Naif like a firm hand in the middle of her back. She took the candle-torch from the wall holder. 'We just need to follow the music.'

She chose a corridor by concentrating on the sound, letting it draw her.

Charlonge followed silently behind her. They passed countless wooden doors pressed into the rock like dates in dough. Behind each one, Naif knew, would be a sparse, nondescript room like the one she had laid in after her Enlightenment. She resisted the desire to look inside any of them, focusing harder as the music grew louder.

'It's here,' she said, finally. She stopped and gave Charlonge the torch. Then she placed her hands to the wall, feeling for a gap or seam.

'But there's no door,' said Charlonge.

Naif bit her lip and let her hands roam the rock further. 'It's behind this wall ... I'm sure.'

'How do we get there?'

Naif turned to the older girl. 'What else did you learn from the books about the monks? Please think hard.'

Charlonge took a nervous breath, glancing over her shoulder. 'How can you be so calm? Joel is like that too.'

'You are capable, Char. Think of all the new ones you've managed. Think of how you've tended me.'

'But this is different. This is forbidden.'

'That's what they want you to believe. Fear traps your mind.' Naif knew that now. It was how Grave worked. Joel had worked that out a long time before her. 'There must be a way through the wall to the music.'

Charlonge pressed a palm to her forehead, thinking. 'The book says that the monks found bones in the tunnels. They drew pictures of them, piled into corners. I suppose that means it was a catacomb before they came.'

'Catacomb?'

'Burial chambers. Crypts.'

Naif knew about crypts too. In Grave they stood amongst the normal dwellings, not separated from the living in the way Suki had described her village's former cemetery. Some of the crypts in Grave were bigger than her house. Inside each one would be a wall of coffin drawers, and near that a pot stand with dried arrangements. Excepting for the Council families. Those crypts – she shuddered – were marble and filled with blank-eyed statues. Those ones had no coffin drawers; each member had their own plot buried beneath the floor of the greeting chamber, marked by a different pattern in the marble mosaic.

She stared at Charlonge with widening eyes. 'You're so clever!'

'Wh-what?'

Naif pointed down and scuffed the smooth floor with her foot. 'The entry is underneath us.'

'Oh, no,' moaned Charlonge, softly. 'Please, no.'

But Naif dropped down on her hands, feeling for the gap, or the hook or the catch. She found it close to the wall in a well-worn groove that was hidden under the rock overhang. She tugged it upward but nothing moved, and the jagged edge grazed her fingers.

'It won't open. I think we should go back,' whispered Charlonge.

But Naif wouldn't give up. She pushed the groove horizontally this time, and a narrow rectangle of floor in front of where she knelt slid open. Markes' music flooded up the stairs.

'Quick, Char.'

But Charlonge stayed still, her back pressed against the wall.

Naif handed her back the torch. 'Stay here and make sure the door stays open. I don't want to be trapped down there.'

She slid her legs over the lip of the opening and eased down onto rough-cut spiral stairs. Descending slowly, she stopped to listen for voices every few steps. The last stair brought her face to face with two thick stone columns. In the gap between them she could see through to a large chamber.

Naif crept to the columns and peered through.

All of the Ripers were in there – not seated at a table as she expected, but standing in a circle. Lenoir had his back to her with Test on one side of him and Graselle –

the only human among them – on the other. Lenoir faced Brand across the circle. Modai stood next to Brand, with Forlorn on the other side.

Further along the wall she saw Markes crouched, clutching his guitar like a shield. Leather cuffs on his ankles were attached to an iron loop and bolted to the floor. Blood streaked his face, and his lips looked puffy and swollen, as if he'd been hit.

The chamber reeked of rage; an acrid, throat-catching taste that billowed around the circle of Ripers like invisible smoke. Naif wanted to wave her arms to clear the air – make it more breathable – but she stayed still, scared to move any further.

Brand stepped into the middle of the circle. 'There's something that should be said before the vote.'

'What is it, Brand? Simply and without decoration, if you please,' said Varonessa. She stood midway between Brand and Lenoir, clearly the arbiter.

'Leyste is dead. Murdered by one of our own.'

The circle of Ripers appeared to writhe like eels caught in a net. But it was Modai who truly frightened Naif. He fell to his knees, clasping his chest as if he'd been stabbed, moaning in a deep and haunted way.

Brand stepped back, her expression showing she was satisfied with the impact of her words.

'Do you claim to know the murderer?' asked Varonessa.

Naif held her breath. What would happen when Lenoir was named?

She became overwhelmed by an urgent need to get out. But the desire wasn't hers; it was Lenoir's. He'd sensed her presence without seeing her and sent her a warning. *Flee*.

She fought against the compulsion and pressed closer to the column. Markes saw her and his face betrayed a mixture of terror and pleading.

Conflicting instincts paralysed her. What would happen to Markes if she left? What would happen to them both if she stayed?

'I killed him, Varonessa,' said Lenoir into the tense quiet.

The Ripers erupted in a clamour of questions and accusations.

'SILENCE!' Varonessa did not raise her voice yet it cut straight through the noise.

Naif felt another surge of power – like bands tightening across her limbs. Someone had taken control of the room, keeping it in order. Either Varonessa or Lenoir.

'Lenoir, explain yourself,' ordered Varonessa.

Lenoir did not move from where he stood. 'Leyste stalked one of the new ones. He saw her arrive at the Register and has been watching her ever since. He tampered with the light relays on a path near Agios and then attacked her.'

'Tampered with the light relays?' Varonessa sounded shocked.

Murmurs rippled around the circle again.

'That is not possible, Lenoir,' said Varonessa.

'Not for one of them,' agreed Lenoir. 'But it is for one of us. One of us assisted Leyste. We cannot let this happen. It's not in our agreement.'

The tension in the chamber threatened to strangle Naif, as if someone had looped a rope over her head and left her to hang. She tried to stop gasping for breath. Someone would hear her. Someone must ...

But the Ripers' attention belonged to Modai. He let out a curdling howl and launched himself at Lenoir.

Lenoir met him chest on and gave a powerful slicing chop into the side of Modai's neck. Modai staggered back, gargling as though his neck were broken. Yet somehow he stayed upright.

The attack brought a rush of release from whoever controlled the chamber and the Ripers leapt at each other. Brand went for Lenoir, Modai for Test in a savage interchange of clawing nails and freakish strength. Screeches filled the cave as the opposing factions tore into each other with the ferocity of wild animals.

Able to breathe again, Naif ran across to Markes and unscrewed the manacles. Neither of them spoke but Naif hooked her shoulder under his and urged him towards the stairs. She resisted looking back for Lenoir in the bloody clash. She would know what happened to him. She would feel it. As she and Markes staggered up the stone steps she sent Lenoir a single thought. *Survive*.

Charlonge met them halfway up. She took Markes's other shoulder and together they helped him up through the sliding trapdoor into the corridor.

'Which way?' said Charlonge.

'I know,' Markes panted, touching the new Circle tattoo on his temple. 'I have an inner map now.'

His clipped directions were the only words that passed between the three of them as they stumbled along the concentric corridors until they reached the main meeting chamber. Jaime had gone but a lone figure waited there, hunched over in the pews.

'Naif!' Suki sprang up and ran over to help. She stared at Markes. 'Pig-cuss! What happened to him?'

'Ripers,' said Naif. 'What's wrong?'

'I've been looking everywhere for you. I went to Vank. Someone saw you and Charlonge take the kar to Syn. When I got here Jaime told me you'd gone to a meeting in the Dominion.' Suki pulled out her knife. 'Had to scare her silly to find that out. She said you wouldn't come back. I told her you could look after yourself. I've been waiting for you.'

Naif's stomach tightened into a cramp of fear. 'Why?'

'Rollo thinks you've been kidnapped by Brand and taken to Danskoi. He's gone off to tell the League. He says they'll find you. That you know someone important in the League.' She bit her lip. 'Do you? Or is he *fou*?'

Naif took a deep breath and glanced at Charlonge. 'He's not *fou*, Suki. My brother Joel ... he's Clash.'

twenty-four

'Your brother is Clash?' Suki gave a low whistle. 'No wonder you didn't want to talk about it.'

'I didn't know until we saw them outside the club when the Night Creatures took that boy.'

'No one goes to Danskoi,' said Charlonge. 'Not even the League. It's forbidden.'

Naif stared at Suki. 'Where did Rollo get that mad idea?'

'That girl of yours,' Suki pointed an accusing finger at Markes. 'She came and told him you'd been taken there.'

'Cal!' said Naif and Markes in unison.

'Why would she do that?' asked Charlonge.

'I told him not to trust her. She's loony over you.' Suki pointed her finger at Markes again. 'She saw you leave the party and thought you'd gone off together somewhere, so she made up a story to get Rollo all crazy worried. She pretended Brand had taken you to Danskoi. If Rollo and the League and the White Wings went there after you, she knew the Ripers would punish them and then the gangs would hate you. She doesn't like the fact that everyone thinks you're a legend.'

'How do you know all that?' asked Naif.

Suki balled her fists and waved them in the air fiercely. 'I know liars. So I waited until they'd gone and I made her tell me the truth.'

Markes looked at Naif. 'I-I'm sorry, I never thought –'

'We've got to stop him,' interrupted Suki. 'The Ripers will take him – all of them.'

'Maybe we can get there before them.'

'Maybe.' Suki's eyes lit with hope.

But Markes began to tremble fiercely, as though shock had finally claimed him. 'The Ripers are down there fighting each other. When they're done they'll kill us all anyway,' he said hoarsely. 'There's nothing anyone can do.'

Naif rounded on him. 'We don't know what will happen. If Lenoir wins then it will be all right.'

And if he doesn't? None of them said it but the question hung heavily between them.

'Suki, can you take Markes to Illi or Agios? He needs *petite nuit* to recover,' said Naif.

Her friend stuck her hands on her hips. 'I want to go with you to find Rollo. I'm not getting stuck with him.'

Markes bit his lip as though he might cry but to Naif's relief he rallied. 'No!' he said. 'I'm not going to rest. Not now. Suki, is it? What have you got on you?'

'You mean *stuff*?'

He nodded.

Suki slipped her hand into her pocket and brought out a pod and some black beads.

'Give me the black ones.'

She shrugged. 'Have you had them before? They jack you pretty high.'

'Good.' He reached forward and picked the beads off her palm. Then he put some in his mouth, holding them on his tongue until they dissolved.

Within a few moments he shook himself free of Naif and Charlonge.

Naif remembered Lottie, dying from burn-out. 'What are you trying to do? Kill yourself?'

'Whatever's happening with the Ripers will change things here forever. And the League's about to break into Danskoi. I'm not going to lie down through the end of Ixion.'

The end of Ixion? Naif's heart thumped harder. *Can it be? Joel and I could leave and go somewhere else. Not Grave, but another place perhaps?* The possibility elated her as much as it scared her.

'I'm coming as well,' whispered Charlonge. 'I want to see Joel.' Tears trickled down her face leaving wet, shiny tracks.

Suki crossed her arms. 'Well, I'm definitely coming because I'm the only one here who knows how to fight.'

They changed lines several times before they reached Los Fien, the highest of the churches. In the kars everyone was talking about the absence of the Ripers.

'Haven't seen a single one this pass,' said a boy sitting in front of Naif and Markes. 'Even that creepy bastard, Modai.'

'I heard they're fighting the League out on the paths,' said another boy, hanging from the aisle straps.

'Not the League,' said the girl sitting closest to him. 'Ruzalia.'

'Whatever,' both guys replied.

'Sssh,' said the girl, noticing Markes. 'It's one of the Circle.'

The boys fell silent and Naif looked at Markes. Sweat stood out on his skin and his eyes glittered in the way that Rollo's had at the Agios ball. His breathing was jerky, but he no longer seemed afraid.

'We have to take the paths from Los Fien and walk up to Danskoi,' he whispered to her, touching his tattoo.

'Have you been there?' she said softly back.

'No. But I heard them talk about it. And I've been to Los Fien. The map will tell me the best way.'

Naif moved her mouth closer to his ear so no one else could hear. 'What happened. How did you end up at the Dominion?'

Markes inclined his head so that they were touching. 'Brand was waiting for me in the apse after I left you outside Agios. She said they needed me to help them catch Ruzalia. She said the time was right – that after the vote she would set it up. I asked what it was they wanted me to do, but Brand wouldn't tell me. I said I wanted to know more and she hit me. She and some other Ripers took me from Agios. They chained me up in the cave until the others came. Then they made me play while they talked. But you came, and the vote never happened.' He spoke in a rush now, the words tumbling out. 'Naif, who is Leyste? What did they mean about the light relays on the path?'

Naif told him what had happened to her.

'But why is Modai so bothered by Leyste's death?'

Naif shook her head slowly. 'I don't know. I've been trying to work that out.'

'We're here!' Suki slapped them both on the shoulders, ending their conversation.

Los Fien appeared the most modest of all the Ixion churches; an unadorned oak construction that reminded Retra of the Grave food warehouses. Raw, metallic music blared through the simply carved entrance doors and only a trickle of partygoers waited on the platform outside to go in.

Markes pointed to lights far above them. The cathedral of Danskoi glowed eerily on the tip of the crater, as if suspended. 'Paths go around either side of Los Fien, and then it's straight up.'

Paths. Panic swelled inside Naif. Without realising, she stopped.

'What is it?' said Markes. 'What's wrong?'

I can't. But she didn't say the words.

'Naif?' Suki peered into her face, frowning. 'You scared or somethin'?'

Unexpectedly, Charlonge spoke up for her. 'A Night Creature has been stalking her since she passed through the Register.' She shifted Suki out of the way and put her arm around Naif's shoulders. 'The creature is dead now, Naif, and it'll be fine as long as we stay on the path.'

Charlonge's confidence revived Naif's courage.

'Yes, you're right,' she said and moved past Markes to take the lead. 'Stay on the path.' She must help Rollo; make up for how she'd treated him.

As they began to climb though, she heard the rustle of movement in the dark and caught a flickering of it in her corner sight. Something watched them.

Behind her, Suki broke a branch from a bush and peeled the spiny leaves off, leaving the sharp stick. She pulled her knife as well.

Markes copied her with the branch.

Naif didn't tell them that a branch would be useless against the Night Creatures. Neither did she tell them, as they reached the last bend in the path before Danskoi, that she knew they were being followed.

They won't come into the light, she told herself. She took care to keep her feet exactly in the middle of the glowing path, concentrating so hard that she failed to see what was ahead of her.

Hands reached from the dark and a cord whipped tight around her throat, pulled by agitated fingers.

'Hush!' said her captor. 'Hush and be still or I'll strangle ye!'

She stopped struggling and strained to turn her head to see the others. Markes lay on the ground, his captor holding his arm twisted and high behind his shoulder, a knee forced into his back. Charlonge was held fast like her, while two of them grappled with Suki.

'She's got a knife,' one of Suki's captors called out.

A boy, nearly as tall as Markes, thrust his face near hers aggressively. 'What're you doing on the high paths? There's business going on up here that's none of yours.'

Naif gagged, trying to answer until he loosened the cord a little, letting her speak.

'If you mean the League, then it's my business too.'

He looked suspicious. 'Why's that?'

'Are you the League?'

He didn't answer.

'Go and tell Clash that his sister is here and needs to talk to him. *Urgently*.'

'If you're lying I'll throw you to them.'

'Them?'

He leaned back so she could see past him to the others and the path along which they'd come. With his free hand he hurled something into the air; a flare that sizzled and then popped as it exploded into light.

The mountainside lit for a long flash with stark white light, bright enough for Naif to see a mass of flesh writhing just beneath the spiny leaves of the bushes. Hundreds of Night Creatures gathered at the edges of the paths, waiting, *craving* for the slip of a foot.

'Brave or stupid are you then?' he whispered. 'If you are truly Clash's sister then I'll go with brave; otherwise I might just give you to them.'

He swung her towards the darkness, lending weight to his taunt.

'No!' shouted Markes.

A tentacle flicked out and snaked around her sore ankle. She kicked but the tentacle tightened and began to drag her from the Leaguer's arms into the dark.

'Cloffie!' admonished a harsh, strong voice. A figure strode in and a sword sliced through the tentacle, freeing Naif's leg.

Cloffie dropped her to the ground.

Naif tore the writhing tentacle from her ankle and got to her feet to face the wielder of the sword. She saw the armour and the wide shoulders and knew immediately who it was.

'Eve.'

'Dark Eve,' corrected the broad, tall girl. She sheathed her sword and peered down into Naif's face. 'Frossing Tri-Suns! It's Clash's little sister! Well, this is an interesting turn of events.' She glanced at the dark as if expecting something more. 'Hurry on. Everyone! This isn't the place for long stories.'

twenty-five

Flanked by Eve and a handful of her League, Naif, Suki, Markes and Charlonge climbed towards Danskoi cathedral.

Ahead, and still a short climb to the cathedral, several paths converged into a nub of clear ground, creating a large pool of light. More Leaguers crouched there, waiting. They faced the dark warily, wearing light bands around their ankles and each carrying a weapon of sorts; sticks or roughly made knives like Suki's.

Naif hurried through the middle of them, to the far side where Joel knelt watching the outside of Danskoi. Heedless of what any of them thought, she flung herself against him. 'Joel, I'm here and I'm all right. Cal lied to Rollo.'

He wore armour of tough, thick leather crudely reinforced with metal plating. It scratched her skin and she recoiled from the large sword strapped to his hips.

'Ret? What're you talking about?' he asked. 'And what're you doing here?'

She tried to quickly order things in her mind to tell him, but it came out in a desperate rushed whisper. 'Suki said that ... Rollo thought I'd been taken by the Ripers to Danskoi. He's joined your League and I thought he'd convinced you to come after me ...'

Naif became aware of all the Leaguers' eyes upon her now – not the dark.

Joel swore and stood up. He hauled Naif out of the circle and half-dragged her up the last segment of the path towards the cathedral.

Eve joined them.

'We're not here because of you, you stupid idiot,' said Joel. 'We've got our own plans and you're not part of them. I told you to stay away – stay with Charlonge.'

'But Charlonge is here to –'

'What?' He swirled and stared back at the others, now herded into the middle of the circle. When he saw Charlonge his expression changed. Naif knew her brother. He was furious and yet … pleased.

Eve saw it too and frowned.

Joel turned back to Naif and grabbed her shoulders. 'You have to go back down the mountain. Take Charlonge with you.'

'No,' said Naif. She shook off his hands. 'I came to Ixion on my own and have lived that way without any help from you. You can't just tell me what to do anymore.'

Joel's eyes widened in surprise. 'But I always have.'

Naif straightened. 'I've always done what everyone told me to do before. Father, the warden, even you. Not anymore, Joel.'

'They can't leave anyway,' Eve intervened. 'The scouts say we're surrounded and I've only got a few flares left. We go in, and what will be, will be.'

'Surrounded? By the Night Creatures?'

Joel and Eve locked gazes and Eve nodded slowly. 'She might as well know, Joel. She's in it now whether she likes it or not.'

'We've been watching Danskoi for a while,' said Joel. 'The Ripers are spending a lot of time up here. And outside it the place is crawling with Night Creatures. The time is right to find out now while the Ripers are distracted.'

'Not just distracted,' said Naif. 'I've come from the Dominion. They never even voted about Ruzalia. Markes and I escaped when they started fighting.'

'The Ripers fighting?' Eve's face came alive.

Naif nodded, swallowing. 'Tearing at each other like beasts. Brand and Modai against Lenoir and Test.'

Joel glanced over at Charlonge, Suki and Markes. 'Markes was with you. Is he the musician? The new Circle member?'

Naif nodded. 'They had him chained to the floor in the Dominion. They planned to use him and Charlonge to lure Ruzalia. They say she covets artists as well as over-agers.'

'And you freed him?' asked Eve.

'After the fighting broke out, no one noticed us.'

'Why didn't they vote?' Eve glanced around as if sensing something again. 'Tell us. *Quickly.*'

Naif felt her urgency; it was as if the oxygen had been sucked from the air, the wind from the night.

At a shouted command from Eve, the Leaguers got to their feet and assembled in fighting stance; knees bent, standing arm's length from each other, pitiful weapons poised. They looked like children playing games, Naif thought, not warriors.

'Brand told the meeting that one of their own had killed a Night Creature called Leyste.' Naif dropped her voice to a whisper, but even that seemed loud in the thickening dark.

'A Riper killed a Night Creature? Is it true?'

Naif nodded again.

'Why should we believe anything you say?' demanded Eve.

'Eve!' admonished Joel. 'My sister might be a nuisance but she doesn't lie.'

A nuisance! Naif wanted to slap him. When had her brother become so arrogant? Or had he always been that way? Full of righteousness and anger?

She raised her leg so that they could see her bruised and bleeding ankle. 'Is that enough proof? Leyste – a Night Creature – stalked me. He attacked me outside Agios after you left me, Joel.' She tried to keep the blame out of her voice.

Eve knelt down to examine the wound. 'It's one of their marks all right. An older one under the fresh blood. How did you get away from it?'

'Lenoir killed it ...'

As soon as she'd uttered the words she wanted to take them back. Not just from the expressions on Eve and Joel's faces, but because a howl went up around them from the dark that turned her bones to paste.

Joel thrust her between him and Eve, and drew his sword.

'Eve?' he said.

'Advance!' bellowed Eve.

The Leaguers ran towards them, two abreast, staying just inside the confines of the narrow path. As they reached Eve and Joel, a freakishly long arm and claw snaked out of the dark and began to drag Cloffie, the leader of the column, from the light. Naif saw the peculiar coils along its muscle and the thick veins pulsating with blood.

Other Leaguers fell upon it, hacking and slashing, but the claw seemed impervious to the blows.

'Clash!' cried Eve.

Joel advanced on the Night Creature, his sword swinging.

The Leaguers retreated as Joel moved in, bringing the sword down with a two-handed chop. He pulled his sword free and swung again, his face so savage, so intense that Naif barely recognised him. She saw her father, though, in the cold fury. This time, his blow severed the claw from the arm and blood sprayed free.

As Joel reached down for the fallen Leaguer the howling intensified and all lights on the path to Danskoi extinguished.

'Get inside the cathedral,' roared Eve above the din. She threw a flare onto the path in front of them and Night Creatures fled its fluorescence. 'Run!' she yelled. 'Run!'

Naif scrambled higher, alongside the Leaguers, losing Joel then glimpsing him again with Charlonge. Markes was next to her for a moment also, forging ahead up the last steep distance to the cathedral.

A small group of Leaguers was already clustered at the door under lantern light. Two of them worked at prying it open while the others watched for attacks.

Eve let go another flare as the larger group converged on the smaller, and everyone milled around the entrance.

'Report!' shouted Eve.

'Wood's too thick to axe,' shouted back the boy who was bent over the lock with only a makeshift hammer and lever.

Naif recognised the voice and pushed her way closer to see him. 'Rollo!' she cried.

He glanced up at her for a moment, his expression surprised and relieved, then returned to gouging the lock.

'Way!' The Leaguers parted, letting Eve through to the door. She knelt down next to Rollo. 'Get it open,' she ordered with quiet imperative. 'My last flare's gone. We can't keep them back.'

Rollo nodded and kept working the huge lock furiously with lengths of twisted metal. Sweat beaded his face, stuck his hair to his head.

Eve pulled her sledgehammer from its sling and walked back to the fringe of the lantern light. The Leaguers closed behind her into a tight, defensive semicircle. The flare light had all but gone. 'Clash!' she bellowed.

Naif pushed past the Leaguers to see Joel join Eve, sword already drawn.

It was just like the first time she'd seen then together behind the club. Only this time their backs were to an unrelenting stone wall and a locked door, and the paths no longer offered escape.

They raised their weapons as the flare finally died and the light shrank back to a tiny pool that barely covered the group. They began to fight the Night Creatures, side by side, with support from the semicircle of Leaguers; swords and batons meeting tentacles and claws.

Lenoir! Help us! Naif concentrated as hard as she could, summoning the sense of bond between her and the Riper. But nothing told her he felt her fear, her need.

'It's loose,' shouted Rollo. 'Just ... a ... little ... long ... er.'
Longer! We need longer!

On impulse Naif ran out to join Joel and Eve, pulling up just short of the reach of their hammer and sword.

'LEYSTE!' she screamed into the dark. 'LEYSTE!'

The howling assault stilled as if the Night Creatures had one listening mind.

With her heart beating in painful thumps, Naif stepped out in front of Joel and Eve.

'I'm the one Leyste stalked. What do you want?' she called into the night. 'Why are you all here?'

'Ret,' whispered Joel. 'Get back –'

'Hush,' she told him softly. 'Rollo is nearly inside ...'

The Night Creatures began to hiss but Naif waved her arms. 'I know you can understand me. I–I'm sorry for Leyste but he'd been following me. Lenoir says it is forbidden for you to do that. Leyste turned off the lights on the path so I would get lost. That is not allowed either.'

The hiss grew until it sounded as though a huge pit of snakes lay before her. She had drawn their attention and they were coming for her now.

'Get back,' she told Joel and Eve. 'Get away from me.' She was going to die here. Even Lenoir couldn't save her this time.

'Look,' shouted Eve. 'Beyond! Lights.'

Torches had appeared on the rough line of the Danskoi path, cutting through the darkness. Lights coming towards them with unshakable intent.

'He's inside,' whispered Joel.

Naif glanced behind. The Leaguers were scrambling inside the church, and Eve and Joel had started taking careful backward steps, weapons raised.

'Come on, Ret,' Joel urged. 'NOW!'

Naif turned and ran for the doors of Danskoi as hard and as desperately as she had run for the Ixion barge.

Claws slashed at her back, catching in her shift and ripping it through. She shrugged out of it and kept going but barbs found her ankle, as if sensing Leyste's mark. They tore the flesh and hooked in the bone.

She collapsed, curling up in pain. *Worse than the obedience strip. Worse than anything.*

'Ret!'

Joel's voice meant nothing.

Even the hammer blow that crushed the creature's skull, releasing her, was a distant event, happening to someone else.

Then someone shook her, sour breath mingling with her own light panting, fierce, demanding eyes in a blunt-featured face, swollen sweat drenching thick skin. 'Are you with us? ARE YOU WITH US?'

'Yes, Eve,' Naif whispered, making her legs work.

Wide lips curled in a smile. 'Good girl.'

Markes held a glow band to her face. 'Open your mouth!' He gave her a strained but genuine smile that only a few passes ago she'd have braved demons to see. Right now it gave her only small comfort. But she did as he said, and he dropped something on her tongue which fizzed. 'I kept one of the beads. In case.'

She tasted the bitter coffee flavour and almost immediately the pain receded, and a vein of energy opened inside her. She sat up and blinked.

The Danskoi narthex was unlit except for the dim glow bands of the Leaguers as they worked frantically to barricade the door with a heavy row of pews.

'We're inside?'

'The other gangs came from behind. Their torches scared the Night Creatures back long enough for us all to get inside.'

'What gangs?'

'The Wings and the Freeks.'

'Kero? Krista-belle?' Her eyes sought them out in the melee, but only found Eve, Joel, Charlonge and Suki on the other side of the entrance hall, trying to lever apart the doors that separated it from the nave.

'You're bleeding,' said Markes.

Naif looked at her ankle. The torn flesh gaped and blood trickled freely, yet she felt detached from the pain.

He untied his bandana from around his neck and tied it around her ankle. 'What you did out there was either the stupidest thing I've ever seen, or the bravest.'

'I ... I knew they would stop and would listen. They're curious about us. And we just needed a few more moments for Rollo to get the door open. Joel and Eve couldn't hold them off.'

Markes shook his head in wonder. 'When Eve tells you to do something you just want to do it. And the way she fights.'

Naif couldn't disagree. She climbed to her feet and hobbled towards the side wall of the narthex. Between pillars she found the narrow opening to the gallery stairs. She began to climb.

Markes followed her. 'I mean,' he stumbled over his words, 'what you did was amazing too. It's just that she does what she believes in – all the time.'

Naif stopped and turned to him. 'And I don't?'

He seemed dazed by her question. 'I-I'm not sure. You don't seem to know what you believe. You're with Lenoir then you're with the League.'

'Well ... what about you? What do you want?'

He lifted his shoulders and shook his head. 'I don't know.'

Naif started climbing again. It wasn't the time for such conversations. More important things weighed on her, drew her.

Like the gallery.

It stretched wider even than Agios but the space was cluttered with the heavy wood furniture that normally occupied the nave. She climbed a table and shifted chairs in order to reach the railing. But then she stopped absolutely still.

'Markes!'

The shock in her voice brought him sliding across the table and straight to her side.

'What?'

Strange floating globes lit the nave below – not candles. They hovered like levia-flies above rows and rows and rows of four-poster beds. A jumbled mass of tubing ran between beds as if connecting them.

'What're you doing up there?' Rollo called from the stairs. When they didn't answer he climbed across to join them.

'I saw you come up here. Naif, where did you ... *oh my fross* ...' He leaned so far over the balcony Naif thought he might fall.

'What do you think it is?' she whispered.

His shook his head. 'It looks like some type of ... distillery for lava?'

'Lava?' said Markes. 'But why all the beds?'

'Not for lava,' said Rollo. He pointed to the figures lying with their limbs entangled on each bed. 'For people.'

twenty-six

'That's just stupid,' said Markes.

But Naif scrambled between the stacked chairs over to the wall hutch where the church binoculars were always kept. One damaged pair lay inside it. She hurried back to Markes and Rollo, fingers shaking as she spun the focus wheel.

'Let me look,' said Rollo, impatiently.

'Wait!' She braced the binoculars against the railing. The image came to her in pieces as she shifted her view. First a girl, anyone, but young like her or Suki or Charlonge, lying still on the bed. The girl seemed peaceful.

She moved the glasses, to the next bed. Another girl. *No.* Someone she knew. *Lottie.*

Naif shifted the glasses lower.

Something clung to the dead girl's cheek. *No, not clinging. Attached.* It was sucking at her skin through a large, puckered crease that could have been a mouth. A tentacle strayed over the girl's neck and chest, stroking tenderly, lovingly.

A Night Creature.

She shifted the glass lower again, expecting to see Lottie's lower torso and legs alongside the curled body of the creature. But as she moved the lens down, their abdomens appeared to be melded together, tapering down to just one set of human legs.

Naif lifted the glass higher again.

Saw Lottie's head and lifeless face.

Across.

The Night Creature's skull shared Lottie's pillow. Pale fluff, the beginning of hair, and the pale pink of new skin intersected by oily flesh. Chests melded as well. Skin merging into skin.

Changing!

Lottie's body was being subsumed into the Night Creature the way a spider would drain an insect.

Naif dropped the glasses in shock and they spun far below to smash on the stone floor.

A globe left its hovering position and skittered across the nave. It shot out a beam of blue light that burned the binoculars where they lay.

Naif turned to Markes and Rollo. 'Stop Eve from forcing the main door open. They mustn't go in there. The globes are weapons. They'll be killed.'

Markes reacted first, throwing himself across the jumble of furniture. Rollo scrambled after him, 'Dark Eve! Dark Eve!'

Naif followed more slowly. Despite taking the black bead, pain shot up her leg every time she put her foot down. It affected her balance and she banged against things. A bubble of nausea pressed up under her ribs. Soon the pain would take over her mind altogether.

She struggled to bring back the lessons she'd learned, separating the pain from the rest of her mind. *Think past it.*

Each step became a miracle of concentration. By the time she reached the first swing of the stairs, hell had disgorged into Danskoi.

The outside door had breached and Night Creatures clamoured over each other to enter.

'Eve!' bellowed Rollo, who was ahead of her. 'Don't open the inside doors!'

But by the time Naif reached the second swing of the staircase she saw the glow of the armed globes pulsing across the narthex like the strobes at the clubs.

The Leaguers and the other gangs were in there, dodging the globes and fighting the tide of Night Creatures trying to enter. Their screams of pain filled the church.

Naif joined Markes against the wall at the bottom stair.

'Over there!' He pointed to Eve and Joel.

Dark Eve and Clash had chopped and slammed their way back towards the outside door. Eve held her shield high with one hand deflecting the beams from the globes, while she wielded her hammer in the other. Joel fought to keep a circle of space around Charlonge and Suki. Suki thrust and slashed with one of Eve's long knives.

'Where are they going?'

'There are lights in the sky outside. I think it's Ruzalia. I can see the echo-locaters.'

Through the open doors Naif glimpsed spotlights wheeling across the ground, sending the Night Creatures scuttling for darker places.

And something else: the outline of a metallic shape on long spidery legs.

Lenoir!

Naif.

'Watch out!' Markes shouted in her ear.

Some of the Leaguers, forced into the corners of the narthex away from the globes, had found the gallery stairs. They began trampling each other to climb them.

Naif and Markes pushed against the rush towards Eve and Joel. They climbed the fallen pews, helping each other over. Screams followed them, and so did the smell of blood.

A Night Creature dropped from the ceiling, knocking Markes to the floor. It attached to his neck like a leech. Markes tried to pull it off but it slipped a tentacle around his neck and tightened it to form a slipped knot.

Markes began to gasp.

'Help!' screamed Naif. Without thinking, she jammed her fingers into the Night Creature's oily maw, trying to break its sucking seal, but it freed another tentacle and wrapped it around her, crushing her against Markes.

'No!'

There was a shout in Naif's ear and something metallic sank deep into the creature's pulpy chest. Its tentacles spasmed then loosened from them both and it fell still at their feet.

Kero and Rollo stood over it, slick with blood, both holding knives.

'Kero, you came? Why?' asked Naif.

'Maybe I just needed someone to show me how to be brave enough,' he replied with a hint of a dangerous grin.

'Where's Krista-belle?'

'Here.' Kero turned and pulled his girlfriend around from behind him where she guarded his back. She was as filthy and bloody as him, and carried a thick piece of wooden railing in her hand.

Naif stepped over the fallen Night Creature and clutched Krista-belle tightly for a moment. 'Thank you,' she whispered.

'Your fight is our fight,' whispered back Krista-belle. She hugged Naif and then moved back close to her boyfriend.

'What're those light things?' asked Kero.

'They're protecting what's inside the nave,' said Naif quickly. 'The church is full of dead or dying Peaks. I recognised one of them.'

Rollo continued for her. 'The Ripers are bringing the Peaks here and having 'em sucked dry.'

'Dry of what?' Kero's voice rose.

'I don't know. But each one has a Night Creature attached. It's like they're using the Peaks to give life to the Night Creatures,' said Naif.

Right then a tentacle shot up from the Night Creature they'd thought was dead and lodged tightly around Krista-belle's throat.

Before anyone could react, her head flopped to one side. She didn't make a sound.

Krista-belle! Naif lost all the sensation in her body.

Kero started from his shock and began to stab the creature with all his force until its body was a mess of severed dark flesh. Then he fell to his knees alongside Krista-belle and wrenched her free from its grip.

Her head lolled against his chest and he roared with rage.

Rollo, who was still holding Markes up, stared, speechless.

'No!' cried Naif.

She went to fall alongside Kero when metallic legs crashed down on either side of her. A door hatch opened abruptly and hands pulled her inside a cocoon of leather and velvet.

Only her.

'Rollo! Markes! Kero!' she rasped. 'Lenoir, don't leave them.'

'Naif, listen to me!' Lenoir's voice stung her out of her daze. She tried to focus on his pale face. 'I'm taking you outside to Ruzalia. You must leave here.'

She tried to make sense of his words but she could only think of the others. 'Not without them,' she screamed.

Lenoir made an angry noise and disappeared.

A few moments later Markes sprawled across the floor of the carriage as if thrown in, followed by Rollo.

Lenoir climbed over him and shook Naif. 'The Night Creatures want your life in return for Leyste's. We won't be able to quell them while you remain here.'

'Where's Kero?'

'He won't leave her and we cannot wait,' snapped Lenoir.

The carriage jerked up on its legs, sending Lenoir sliding across the seat into her. Markes and Rollo crashed into the opposite door. Then it tossed them all back the other way as it juddered across the narthex out into night.

Through the window she saw the sky now swarming with levia-fly trails as they buzzed protection around the bulky lines of a zeppelin. The zeppelin's incandescent spotlights had converged on a single spot, giving protection to a small group of figures.

The spider took them straight to Joel and Eve on the path beneath the balloon-ship. Naif saw Joel swaying, barely able to stand. Charlonge gripped him around the waist, helping him stay upright. But Eve still prowled the edges of the light, swinging her hammer at the Night Creatures.

The carriage stopped on the edge of the pool of light and re-folded its legs. Lenoir opened the door of the carriage and leapt out.

Eve spun towards him and her hammer lifted menacingly. Her intention spurred Naif to climb out. 'Eve! Stop!'

Rollo helped Markes follow her.

'Look!' shouted Joel, pointing.

The five of them stopped and stared up at the platform descending from the belly of the zeppelin.

Joel pointed his blood-wet sword at Lenoir. 'What do you want with my sister?'

'To keep her alive,' said Lenoir. 'I can't restore order among the Night Creatures while she stays in Ixion. She's the cause of their distress.'

Eve lowered her hammer and shield at his admission. Sweat poured down her bare arms. 'Why are ... you helping ... us?' she panted.

'She's not one of you,' said Lenoir. 'She's bonded to *me* and I'll do much to ensure her safety.'

'Bonded!' spat Joel. 'You've perverted her!'

'Call it what you like but she's alive. Either she leaves now or the Night Creatures or the renegade Guardians will harm her. Her badge has been revoked. It was the only way I could keep my majority. Varonessa insisted.'

Naif looked at her palm. The oily badge had turned a charcoal colour and had begun to peel. 'You were fighting ... Modai and Brand. What happened?'

'Modai is injured. But he and Brand escaped and are hiding.' He stared into the dark as if expecting them to appear. 'If you wish everyone here to be safe then you and the musician must leave now. I will only be able to subdue the Night Creatures when you're gone. Hurry.'

The platform dangled only a short distance above them now.

'Clash,' said Eve. 'Talk to her.'

Joel limped over to Naif. 'Go please, Ret,' he said. 'You never wanted to come here anyway. It was just for me.'

'Wait, where's Suki?' cried Rollo suddenly.

Charlonge began to cry. 'She fell at the door. I couldn't pick her up, and then I lost sight of her when everyone pushed to get out. Naif, I'm sorry. I don't know if she's still ... alive.'

Suki. Naif wanted to run out into the dark and find her friend.

But Eve grabbed hold of the swaying platform and steadied it. She waved up at the figures peering from the zeppelin's under-cabin. 'Get on. Both of you. Now!'

'Lenoir lied to me,' she said to them all as she helped Markes aboard.

'What lie?' the Riper protested.

She felt his desire for her to leave there, like fingers squeezing her flesh, but beneath that was honest puzzlement.

'The Peaks. You said it was better. A better place that they went to.'

'But it is.' And he believed that. She knew.

'Did you see inside Danksoi?' she asked Eve and Joel.

Joel shook his head. 'As soon as we got the doors open the globe things attacked and then Ruzalia came. We never got inside.'

'It looks like they're using the Peaks to *grow* the Night Creatures,' said Naif.

'What do you mean?' demanded Eve.

'It is part of our process,' said Lenoir.

'What process?'

But Lenoir cut Eve off as a tentacle lashed at them from the dark. 'There is no time for this!'

Naif turned to Joel and reached out with both arms. 'Come with us,' she begged.

'No, Ret, I need to stay here. The fight isn't over.' He leaned over the edge of the platform and hugged her. 'I'm proud of you. You're not the person I thought you were and I'm glad. Be safe,' he whispered. Then he let go of her and took Charlonge's hands. 'Char, you can't stay either.'

'Joel's right, Char. Withdrawal is death.' Naif looked at Joel. 'Everyone must know that. Tell them all. Promise me.'

'I promise,' he said and helped Charlonge onto the platform. 'And you must tell Ruzalia what you've seen in Danskoi.'

Naif nodded, then beckoned Lenoir close to her so she could lean down close to his ear. 'Tell me why the Night Creatures blame me for Leyste's death?'

His expression changed. She saw the sadness again; felt it blanket her like a fall of snow. 'Because I am one of them, and they do not kill their own: even a transformed one who has harmed them. So it's you they must blame,' he said softly. He took hold of her hand and kissed it in a desperate way.

Naif's head spun with confusion. Lenoir had lied. Or had he? If the Night Creatures were somehow using the Peaks to transform into Ripers then maybe, to Lenoir, they *were* going to a better place.

But she had no chance to ask him more. The platform jerked upward as its ropes began to rewind, pulling her from his grasp.

'Naif,' called out Rollo.

'Find Suki,' she called back. 'Find her for me, Rollo.'

Ruzalia waited by the under-cabin's window, her face hidden by impenetrable eye-shades. Her thick, red hair – the same colour as Rollo's – was knotted at the nape of her neck like rope.

'Take that one to the healer,' she ordered, placing a lit cigar between her lips.

A serious-looking girl dressed in light armour helped Markes through a partition, to the opposite end of the cabin.

Puffing smoke, Ruzalia sank into a large armchair and motioned for Naif and Charlonge to sit opposite her. 'So which of you is the cause of all this trouble?'

'I am,' said Naif without preamble. 'The Ripers are divided because Lenoir killed one of the Night Creatures to protect me.'

Ruzalia leaned forward. 'You? How fascinating. Why would the leader of the Guardians do that?'

Naif met Ruzalia's penetrating stare with a steady gaze. 'That is not important right now. I have a message for you from Eve and Clash. We've seen inside Danskoi. The Ripers are using the Peaks to make new Night Creatures.'

Ruzalia slapped her thigh in anger. 'Danskoi. Right beneath my nose all along. I knew some perverted doings were at hand, but had no proof of it.'

The three gazed from Ruzalia's viewing window as the levia-flies engaged the globes in a clash of light beams. Globes ignited and dropped like fiery comets to the ground. In their dying light, Naif could see more Ripers swarming up from Los Fien towards Danskoi in metal carriages, racing towards Lenoir and the others.

Then the zeppelin lifted and swung away.

The wrench of leaving Ixion faded a fraction as the light trails blended with the glittering luminosity from the clubs and majestic churches, transfixing her. Beautiful.

'Hold tight,' said Ruzalia.

The zeppelin lifted again, so quickly this time that Naif's stomach felt as if it had been pitched outside her body. She gripped her chair and pressed her forehead to the window-glass, swallowing against the unpleasant sensation. Nothing but darkness below and above, and the vanishing lights of Ixion.

Where are we going to in this endless night?

Ruzalia leaned forward and dropped a translucent mask on her and Charlonge's laps. 'Quickly. Put it on.'

Charlonge obeyed instantly but Naif stared at the mask with suspicion.

A moment later, as brilliant daylight and Ruzalia's laughter exploded upon her senses, she clamped her eyes shut and fumbled for it. She waited for the eye pain to subside before she dared to open them again and peer out through the mask's filter.

The radiance of the sky and water made it hard to distinguish one from the other and for a moment she wondered if they were upside down. Then she saw a stretch of little green shapes – islands spaced apart as though they'd been sprinkled upon the ocean carpet by a giant hand.

She closed her eyes against the assault of light and colour and rested back in her seat while, next to her, Charlonge wept with sadness and relief.

A notion came to Naif then, born of anguish and anger and sorrow at what she'd left behind her; a thought emerging from her confusion. 'Ruzalia, is it possible that the Ripers may not be the creators of what is happening in Ixion, but are caught in a trap of their own?'

Ruzalia crushed her cigar into a metal ashtray on the arm of chair and crossed her legs. She leaned back and blew rings into the air between them. 'You pose an interesting question, youngling.'

Naif sank her face into her hands, exhausted with pain and sick with possibilities. 'I have a friend called Rollo. He saw a Riper in Grave talking to a Councillor.'

'Indeed?' The pirate woman leaned forward, lighting another cigar. 'Did your friend hear their conversation?'

Naif shook her head. 'No.' Saying it aloud gave her a surge of purpose. 'But I will find out.' *For Rollo. For Kristabelle. For all of them. I will find out and come back.* 'Ruzalia, please can you take me back to Grave?'

About the Author

Marianne de Pierres is the award-winning author of the Parrish Plessis and Sentients of Orion science fiction series. Marianne is an active supporter of genre fiction and has mentored many writers. She lives in Brisbane, Australia, with her husband, three sons and three galahs. She also writes award-winning humorous crime novels under the pseudonym, Marianne Delacourt.

acknowledgements

This book has taken me several years to write. It's a book I felt so passionate about that I kept working on it despite contracts for other novels. Many people have been a part of *Burn Bright* and I'd like to send them all my heartfelt thanks. Firstly, to Tara Wynne, my agent, who loved it right away even when it was just a one paragraph idea. My writers group ROR, who encouraged me to continue with it after they saw a skeleton draft (Tansy Rayner Roberts for her excitement, Dirk Flinthart for suggestions about the gangs, and Margo Lanagan who said it was full of de Pierres 'yummies', Richard Harland, Rowena Cory Daniells, Trent Jamieson and Maxine McArthur for the *thumbs up*).

Special thanks go to my publisher, Zoe Walton, who saw potential in the manuscript and gave a lot of extra time to help me re-work it into something much better. Zoe, I will never be able to thank you enough! Then there's the Random House team. WOW! What can I say? You have been truly amazing. Peri Wilson, Sarana Behan, Justin Ractliffe, Linsay Knight – a gift to this veteran adult fiction writer venturing nervously into new territory.

I'd also like to mention my early readers, Ruth Cohen and Amy Parker, who gave invaluable feedback. And the

Burn Bright Staffies who've been working so hard to make the website a vibrant place to visit long before the book entered the world.

Finally, a huge thank you to Yunyu for wanting to play in my world and inviting me to play in hers.

I hope *Burn Bright* does you all proud.

Printed in Great Britain
by Amazon.co.uk, Ltd.,
Marston Gate.